RAIDERS OF THE
RIO GRANDE

DATE DUE

JAN 1 7 2007		
JAN 1 9 2007		
FEB 0 6 2007		
MAR 2 0 2007		
APR 1 9 2007		
ming 5/2007		
JUN 0 5 2007		
MAY 2 7 2009		
JUN 0 8 2009		
JUL 2 7 2010		
GAYLORD		PRINTED IN U.S.A.

Raiders of the Rio Grande

Bradford Scott

WHEELER
CHIVERS

This Large Print edition is published by Wheeler Publishing, Waterville, Maine, USA, and by BBC Audiobooks Ltd, Bath, England.
Wheeler Publishing is an imprint of Thomson Gale, a part of The Thomson Corporation.
Wheeler is a trademark and used herein under license.
The text of this Large Print edition is unabridged.
Other aspects of the book may vary from the original edition.
Set in 16 pt. Plantin.

LIBRARY OF CONGRESS CATALOGING-IN-PUBLICATION DATA

Scott, Bradford, 1893–1975.
    Raiders of the Rio Grande / by Bradford Scott.
        p. cm.
    ISBN 1-59722-387-5 (lg. print : pbk. : alk. paper) 1. Large type books.
I. Title.
PS3537.C9265R35 2006
813'.54—dc22   2006029060

BRITISH LIBRARY CATALOGUING-IN-PUBLICATION DATA AVAILABLE

Published in 2006 in the U.S. by arrangement with
Golden West Literary Agency.
Published in 2007 in the U.K. by arrangement with Golden West Literary Agency.

U.S. Softcover: ISBN 13: 978-1-59722-387-4; ISBN 10: 1-59722-387-5
U.K. Hardcover: 978 1 405 63994 1 (Chivers Large Print)
U.K. Softcover: 978 1 405 63995 8 (Camden Large Print)

Printed in the United States of America on permanent paper
10 9 8 7 6 5 4 3 2 1

RAIDERS OF THE RIO GRANDE

1

Loco Lobo rode out of Laredo with lead whistling about his ears, lead that did not connect. Behind him he left two dead men sprawled in the dust, their glazing eyes glaring up stonily at the blue of the Texas sky.

One was the manager of Jimson's big general store, the other a Mexican policeman — Laredo's police department composed in equal numbers of Mexicans and Americans.

Loco Lobo held up Jimson's in broad daylight. At gunpoint, he forced the manager to open the safe, which contained the week's take, several thousand dollars. He scooped out and sacked the money and backed to the door and his waiting horse, warning the manager to stay where he was and not make a noise.

The manager used the bad judgment of ignoring the warning and following Loco Lobo out the door, shouting for help. The nearby policeman heard his cries and rushed to his aid. Loco Lobo turned in his saddle and drilled both dead center with two shots; Loco Lobo never missed.

Two other policemen, witnessing the killings from a distance, opened fire, but Loco Lobo escaped unscathed, left town by way of Santa Rita Avenue and vanished into the brush country north and west of Laredo.

Sheriff Tobe Medford and his deputies saddled up in hot haste and rode in pursuit, with negative results. Loco Lobo knew the brush country as he knew the palm of his hand and easily eluded the pursuers. The disgusted posse rode back to town under the stars.

The following afternoon, another day of golden sunshine, Ranger Walt Slade, named by the Mexican *peones* of the Rio Grande River villages *El Halcón* — The Hawk — rode south by east along the lonely river trail, through a desolate and sparsely settled area. To the north and west, the brush-covered rangeland, smoldering with the purple sage, swept to distant horizons. To the south and east was the turbulent flood of the Rio Grande.

Lounging easily in the saddle, Slade sang softly to himself in his deep and richly musical voice. He felt cheerful and carefree and looked forward to Laredo and some days and nights of relaxation and diversion, both welcome after a long and hard ride. And now Laredo wasn't so very many miles off. But just the same he rode watchful and alert.

Suddenly Shadow, his magnificent black horse, snorted and blew softly through his nose. Slade instantly became even more watchful, his extraordinarily keen eyes sweeping the terrain in every direction. Glancing over his shoulder, he spotted five horsemen some six or seven hundred yards behind. They rode purposefully and it seemed to Slade their gaze was fixed on himself.

Nothing so unusual about that, however; quite likely just a troop of cowhands headed for town. But on this lonely trail, it behove a lone rider to be watchful; things happened on the river trail, not all of them nice. And it seemed to Slade the horsemen were closing the distance. He spoke to Shadow and the big black lengthened his stride. Another glance told Slade the followers had also speeded up. Still nothing so very unusual. Nevertheless, he shifted the reins, reached down and made sure his high-power Winchester was free in the saddle boot. That gun was a "special" procured for him by

James G. "Jaggers" Dunn, the General Manager of the great C. & P. Railroad System, who had a habit of getting whatever he went after, be it a rifle or a corporation. Slade glanced back again. And even as he did so, a puff of smoke mushroomed from the ranks of the following riders. A bullet sang by overhead, not too close.

"So!" Slade exclaimed aloud. "Want to play rough, eh? Well, odds of five to one are a bit lopsided, and besides I still don't know what it's all about, so we won't take part in the game, just yet. Let's go, Shadow!"

The big black lunged forward. More slugs whined past, but still not too close, the distance being too great for anything like accurate shooting from the back of a galloping horse.

And then abruptly things got altogether too interesting. From the brush some five hundred yards ahead bulged two more riders who reined in and opened fire at the advancing horseman, their bullets coming altogether too close for comfort.

Caught in a deadly cross-fire, it looked like curtains for the lone horseman.

But not for "the fastest and most accurate gunhand in the whole Southwest." Slade let the knotted reins fall on the horse's neck, whipped the Winchester from the boot and clamped it to his shoulder. His voice rang out —

"Steady, Shadow!"

Instantly the black horse leveled off on a smooth running walk that hardly jolted his rider. Down came the front sight into the notch, until it was but a gleaming point of light. The heavy rifle belched flame and smoke. One of the riders lurched far back on the crupper and slid to the ground to lie motionless. An answering slug whipped through the crown of Slade's hat. Bullets from behind were hissing all around him.

Again the Winchester boomed, and there were two figures lying motionless on the ground. Slade's voice rang out again —

"Trail, Shadow, trail!"

A mighty forward leap and the black horse was fleeing like a cloud before a lightning flash. Slade hunched far forward in the hull as lead whined past. For a moment it was touch-and-go, then the bullets no longer came close. Shadow was leaving the pursuing horses behind as if they were standing still. Slade muttered wrathfully and slipped two fresh cartridges into the magazine. The Winchester ready for instant action, he wasted but a single glance at the bodies as he swept past, deeming it not wise to linger with the horsemen behind still thundering in futile pursuit.

"Well, a nice reception committee," he growled. "Same old section, horse, not a bit different from the last time we were here. Let's go, I'm hungry." His glance swept the terrain ahead, the big rifle still ready for business, although he thought it unlikely other drygulchers were holed up in the brush, waiting. He risked a quick glance back. The pursuing riders, now out of rifle range, were grouped about the bodies.

With the sun nearing the western horizon, Slade reached the cultivated area where the great irrigation project that would eventually turn the valley into a garden spot was going strong. A project, incidentally, in the successful consummation of which Walt Slade had played no small part. Now he rode past flourishing crops and trim little farmhouses where children played and laughter sounded. Here were happiness and prosperity and Slade felt the dangers and hardships he had encountered in the course of his previous visits to the section had been well worth while. He rode on, uplifted, and forgot about what had happened farther west.

Walt Slade rode into Laredo by way of Santa Rita Avenue. Behind him he left two dead men sprawled in the dust, their glazing eyes glaring up stonily at the blue of the Texas sky!

2

Turning east on Montezuma Street, Slade approached San Bernardo Avenue where he knew was a small hotel favored by cattlemen and a dependable stable. First he cared for Shadow. The old stable keeper remembered both man and horse and had a warm greeting for them. Knowing Shadow would get the best of care, the keeper having previously been properly introduced to the big black — a one-man horse — Slade repaired to the hotel and registered for a room, in which he deposited his saddle pouches. Then he made his way to the sheriff's office.

Tobe Medford was sitting at his desk composing a letter when Slade entered, and he looked to be in anything but a good temper. But as he recognized his visitor, his face became radiant.

"Walt!" he whooped, leaping to his feet and extending his hand. "If you don't beat all! I was just writing Captain McNelty, asking for a few dozen Rangers to straighten things out, but I reckon you'll do instead."

Slade sighed resignedly. "I'm supposed to be on vacation, as much on vacation as a Ranger can ever be," he replied. "I was riding down here for a visit with the Telo family, Marie, Rosa, and Estaban, Rosa's husband, and barge right into a ruckus."

"How's that?" the sheriff asked. Slade told him. Medford indulged in some weird profanity.

"Some of Loco Lobo's bunch, sure as blazes!" he exclaimed. "They pulled that sort of thing before. A couple of cowhands were murdered for their horses and what they had in their pockets — payday money. A third had his horse shot from under him and escaped into the brush and told how they work it. So you did for two of the sidewinders, eh? Fine! Fine! Guess they didn't know they were bucking *El Halcón,* or they wouldn't have tried it."

"Possibly not," Slade conceded. "Cowhands as a rule don't pack rifles, and at five hundred yards or more they are generally not very good shots." He repeated the sheriff's initial statement, "Loco Lobo? Bad Spanish for mad wolf."

"May be bad Spanish, but he's a mad

15

wolf, all right, and he's bad. Just about the worst that's showed up in this section, which is saying plenty, as you know," growled the sheriff. "Hyderphobia skunk would be better; he's all of that. Got me running around in circles like a fool dog chasing his tail, and getting nowhere."

"What's on your mind, Tobe?" Slade asked.

The sheriff, his account liberally interspersed with cuss words, related the details of the outrage the day before.

"Both good men," he concluded. "Jimson's manager was a swell jigger, and that poor flatfoot was okay."

Slade nodded. "Can you give me a description of your amigo, *El Lobo Loco?*"

"Guess I can," Medford replied. "When he robbed the bank at Zapata and killed a clerk and the cashier, another clerk was hiding in a back room and escaped and got a good look at him. Said he was a big tall hellion with a dark face that sorta ran to nose, and black hair. Was that clerk who hung that fool name on him, I reckon. Said when he shot the cashier, his lip pulled up over his teeth in a reg'lar wolf-snarl grin. Name fits."

"Did the clerk notice how he was dressed?"

"Said him and the three devils with him

16

— another one stayed outside with the horses — wore rangeland duds. Oh, I expect he was a cowhand once, can't say for sure. We're getting all sorts here since the irrigation project got going strong, thanks largely to you, and folks began pouring in."

"Did they make much of a haul?" Slade asked.

"They sure did," Medford answered. "Seems there was a big deposit made that day for the use of a fellow who aimed to buy land."

"And Loco Lobo learned about it?"

"Looks sorta that way," Medford admitted. "Either that or he was darn lucky in the day he picked for his holdup. What do you think?"

"I would say," Slade replied thoughtfully, "that your Loco Lobo has connections of some sort here in town that inform him where there is opportunity for a lucrative haul. I gather from your description that he is an individual of rather striking appearance, who would stand out in a crowd, so it is unlikely that he would show up in Laredo, except perhaps at some of the shadier rumholes down around the river, or in Nuevo Laredo across the river in Mexico."

"Does sorta look that way," the sheriff conceded. "Sure seems to always know where to hit it rich. When he held up the Catarina stage and killed the driver and the guard, that coach was packing a lot more *dinero* than usual, and I gather that there was more cash than average in the Jimson store safe yesterday. Yes, you could be right. But who the devil could be tied up with the sidewinder here in town?"

"A question to which it is important to get the answer," Slade said. "And very likely getting it won't be easy. Another example of the new type of criminal invading the West, as I've mentioned before. A close-knit organization with a ruthless field man to pull the actual chores, with somebody, doubtless with a respectable front, staying under cover and directing operations. Remember, that is how it worked out the last time I was here."

"Which means we've got more than one horned toad to run down," growled Medford.

"I regard it quite probable," Slade agreed. "Well, we'll see."

"And anyhow you made a start darn fast," said Medford. "More than anybody else has been able to do. But don't forget, Loco Lobo is going to be looking for you."

"Let him look," Slade replied carelessly. "Perhaps he'll look the wrong way for a second." Medford chuckled, understanding perfectly what *El Halcón* meant.

"Yep, that'll be all the time you'll need," he said. "Now what?"

"Now," Slade answered, "I hanker for something to eat; been quite a while since breakfast."

"I'm in favor of it," said Medford. "The Montezuma?"

"Sure," Slade replied. "I like the Montezuma, and Gorty, the owner. Besides, sooner or later most everybody shows up at the Montezuma. Might note something of interest.

"By the way," he added casually, "is Marie Telo still working for Miguel Sandoval, in his cantina down toward the bridge?"

"Yep, she's still working there," Medford said. "Of course, as you know, she doesn't need to work; she's well fixed since they sold the river bottom acres of their ranch to the irrigation people for a whoppin' big price, the ranch the Land Committee hellions stole and you got back for her and her sister Rosa, Estaban's wife. No, she don't need to work, but Marie isn't the sort of gal to sit around the ranchhouse and do nothing. Besides, she says Miguel needs her to keep his book work in order, and she likes to dance and spends a good part of her time

19

on the floor. What say, shall we mosey there after we eat?"

"A good notion," Slade agreed. "First, though, after we finish eating, I want to run over to my hotel room and freshen up a bit; I can stand it."

"Oh, you'd do all right as is," declared the sheriff. "Those bristles become you. Make you look real distinguished. Like —"

"A porcupine with the itch," Slade finished the sentence. "Let's go!"

The Montezuma was the same as the last time Slade visited it — big, brightly lighted, noisy and crowded. With its long, shining bar, its back bar pyramided with bottles of every shape and color, its dance floor, roulette wheels, faro bank, tables for card games, and others for diners who preferred leisurely eating to grabbing a snack at the spotlessly clean lunch counter.

John Gorty, the rubicund owner, his face wreathed in smiles, came hurrying across the room, hand outstretched.

"Mr. Slade!" he exclaimed. "This is a most welcome surprise and calls for a mite of celebration. Sit down! Sit down! First one on the house, from my private bottle. How are you, Mr. Slade? You look fine, and it's sure fine to have you with us again. Howdy, Tobe, take a load off your feet. You spavined old coots hadn't oughta stand too long: liable to topple over."

"Shut up, you lard tub!" replied the sheriff. "I'll be one of your pall bearers." Gorty chuckled and hurried to fetch the bottle, a waiter obliging with glasses.

They enjoyed a leisurely and satisfying dinner, Slade meanwhile studying faces, his keen ears catching scraps of conversation, but learning nothing he considered of interest. Finally he pushed back his empty plate and rolled a cigarette. The sheriff hauled out his pipe and ordered another snort. Slade settled for a final cup of coffee.

"Quite a few new faces," he commented.

"Yes, the old pueblo is building up," Medford replied. "Already calling itself a city. Just the same, she's still a heck-raising frontier town and getting woolier all the time."

Suddenly the swinging doors slammed open and two excited cowhands rushed in. They glanced about, spied Medford and sped to the table.

"Sheriff, got something to tell you," one gasped. "Figured you'd want to know. About seven miles to the west of here a couple of jiggers are layin' in the trail. Nope, they ain't asleep, or if they are, it'll be a devil of a time 'fore they wake up. Drilled

21

dead center, both of 'em. Looks like they had a falling out over something and did for each other. We didn't look close, gave 'em a quick once-over and rode on. Figured it wasn't a good idea to hang around. Didn't know for sure what was going on. Mean lookin' cusses." He paused expectantly.

"Okay, Wilbur," said the sheriff composedly. "Much obliged for bringing me the word. I'll mosey over there tomorrow and pick up the carcasses, if the coyotes don't beat me to them. Guess they'll stay right where they are."

"Yes, guess they will," the cowboy returned dryly. "Looked sorta tired." He and his companion hurried to the bar and began talking excitedly to a group that soon surrounded them.

"Guess their guess is good as any, eh?" the sheriff remarked to Slade.

"Yes," Slade decided. "They'll spread the yarn all around and it may cause somebody else to do some guessing. Yes, we won't contradict their surmise. I'll ride with you tomorrow. Now I'm going to clean up a bit; see you in half an hour."

In his room, Slade quickly bathed, shaved, and donned a spare shirt and overalls his saddle pouches contained. With a final glance at his reflection in the bureau mirror, he tipped his hat at a jaunty angle and returned to the Montezuma.

"All set to amble down to Miguel's cantina?" Medford asked.

"Guess we could do worse," Slade replied.

They walked warily on their way down town, but arrived at Miguel's place without incident.

The big cantina was just as crowded as the Montezuma but less noisy. The lighting was subdued, the furnishings in good taste, a really excellent Mexican orchestra played muted music. At the moment, Miguel himself was not in evidence. The crowd was composed of mostly Mexicans and Mexican-Texans, with a fair sprinkling of cowhands, and business people from uptown, Miguel's being a universal favorite.

As they entered, Slade immediately glanced toward the dance floor. His eyes centered on a girl dancing with a rotund young cowhand who appeared quite enamored with his pretty partner. She was slender and graceful, and small. Her figure, Slade thought, was just about perfection. She had great sloe eyes, a creamily tanned complexion, and black, curly hair as glossy as a raven's wing in the sunlight. Her lips were vividly red and sweetly turned. The light reflected back in kaleidoscopic sparkles from the spangles on her short dancing skirt.

She seemed to sense his regard, for suddenly she turned and glanced in his direction, said something to her dance partner, slipped from his embrace, and fairly flew across the room.

"Darling!" she exclaimed, holding out both little hands, over which Slade bowed with courtly grace.

"So you did come back!" she said, in her soft, musical voice. "You're here!"

"Unless I'm in Heaven and seeing angels," he replied. Miss Marie Telo shrugged daintily.

"So!" she said, "the girls have taught you how to say pretty things."

"What girls?" he retorted, striving to look indignantly innocent and succeeding not at all. Marie tossed her gleaming curls.

"How should I know which one," she said. "But what matters one among so many! Wait, I'll fetch Miguel from the back room; he also will be overjoyed to see you." She skipped gaily across the room and opened a door, through which she vanished from sight. Slade and the sheriff occupied a vacant table.

At the bar, the young cowboy who had been her dance partner was solacing himself with a drink.

"Always the way," he sighed to a companion. "It's the big square-jawed jiggers who gets 'em. But even if he did grab my girl from me, ain't he one heck of a fine looking feller?"

"Sure is," the other agreed. "Don't think I ever saw a finer."

The two hands were not far off. Walt Slade was very tall, more than six feet, with shoulders and chest slimming down to a lean sinewy waist that matched his splendid height. A rather wide mouth, grin-quirked at the corners, relieved somewhat the tinge of fierceness evinced by the prominent hawk nose above and the powerful jaw and chin beneath. The sternly handsome countenance was dominated by long, black-lashed eyes of very pale gray, cold, reckless eyes that nevertheless always seemed to have little devils of laughter lurking in their clear depths.

His homely rangeland garb — bibless overalls, soft blue shirt with vivid handkerchief looped at the throat, scuffed half-boots of softly tanned leather, and broad-brimmed "J.B." — enhanced rather than detracted from his distinguished appearance. No matter how he was dressed, Walt Slade *wore* his clothes; they did not "wear" him.

Marie reappeared from the back room with big, jolly Miguel Sandoval, the owner, in tow, smiling delightedly. He embraced Slade with Latin effusiveness, patting his back and shoulders and greeting him in both colloquial English and colloquial Spanish, with a few pungent Yaqui Indian expletives thrown in for good measure.

"Ha! A day to remember!" he exclaimed. "The wine for Marie, the strong waters for the sheriff, the coffee, I suppose, for Mr. Slade. All will be forthcoming without delay, and with you I will drink." He beckoned a waiter, rattled off a string of orders; the waiter hurried to fill them.

"And, *Capitan*, we trust you will remain with us for some time," remarked Miguel, sampling his glass.

"He's supposed to be on vacation and came to pay us a visit, but of course he had to get mixed up in a shindig right away," put in the sheriff.

"How was that?" asked Miguel.

The sheriff retold Slade's account of his brush with the drygulchers, adding his own coloring of the affair. Marie clenched her little fist.

"I wish I had been with you," she said to Slade.

"Well, it would have sort of evened the odds a bit," he admitted. "You sure came in handy once before, when your fast thinking and straight shooting saved me from an owl-hoot's bullet."

"And I'd do it again," she declared. Slade gazed at her with admiration. Although Texas born, as was her father before her, she was nevertheless a true daughter of the Telos, that illustrious family that for centuries was the bar on the northern gate of Spain.

Miguel and the sheriff wandered to the bar for a word with acquaintances, leaving Slade and Marie at the table.

"I'm sending word to Rosa and Estaban that you're here," she said. "They'll ride to town right away."

"And you still live here, in the little house with the garden and the flowers?"

"Yes," she replied.

"Alone?" crinkling his eyes at her.

"Yes, alone with — memories."

"Memories translate to realities," he reminded her.

"I hope so," she replied softly, lowering her lashes.

3

The following day, about mid morning, Slade and the sheriff rode west on the river trail. Accompanying them were two deputies leading a couple of mules to accommodate the bodies of the slain drygulchers. Medford and the deputies chatted animatedly as they rode, but Slade was unusually silent, his black brows drawing together slightly, his eyes constantly scanning the terrain ahead.

Finally they came to the foot of a long and low rise, beyond the crest of which lay the bodies. Half way up, Slade called a halt.

"Here we turn into the brush and circle around," he announced.

"Why?" asked one of the deputies.

"Because it would appear we are up against a shrewd and far-seeing devil who misses no bets," Slade replied. "Just possible that a trap might be set for us. Now keep quiet from here on."

Slowly and carefully they threaded their way through the chaparral, which was much denser here to the north than across the trail toward the river. Finally Slade again called a halt.

"Here we leave the horses and the mules and hope they keep quiet," he said. "Can't take a chance on the racket they make pushing through the growth. All this may be needless, but somehow I have a hunch it isn't."

"And your blasted hunches most always pay off," growled Medford, under his breath.

"Tie your horses and the mules," Slade ordered, dropping the split reins to the ground — all that was needed to keep Shadow right where he was until called for.

The order was quickly obeyed and they stole toward the trail, not much more than a hundred yards distant, on foot. They had covered little more than half the distance when Slade paused, sniffing sharply.

"Somebody there ahead," he breathed. "Somebody who has lighted a cigarette. Slow and careful, now. For Pete's sake, don't make a noise, and keep your eyes open; I think the hunch is going to pay off. You do the talking, Tobe; we have to give them the chance they don't deserve to surrender. I don't think they will, so shoot fast and shoot straight. Let's go!"

At a snail's pace they continued their progress, peering, listening, nerves stretched to the breaking point in anticipation. The deputies started as to their ears came the sound of low voices directly ahead. Slade, in the lead, slowed the pace still more.

A few more creeping yards, with the trail close, and they sighted two men lounging at the edge of the growth, gazing eastward. Slade started to nod to the sheriff.

And at that moment, one of the mules, the most unpredictable of critters, cut loose with a raucous bray.

The two drygulchers whirled in the direction of the sound, going for their guns. Weaving, ducking, slithering, Slade drew and shot with both hands. Answering slugs grained the flesh of his upper arm, ripped through the leg of his overalls. The sheriff's and the deputies' guns thundered an echo.

Under the hail of lead, the two outlaws fell like grain beneath the sickle, to lie motionless. The deputies started forward.

"Hold it!" Slade halted them. "Keep quiet, there might be some others around somewhere."

For moments they stood motionless and silent, Slade straining his ears to catch the slightest sound.

But only the chirping of birds in the thickets broke the silence. There was no sign of movement amid the growth.

"Guess those are all," Slade said, nodding toward the bodies as he reloaded his guns. "Let's see what's in the trail."

Lying where he had left them the day before were the two outlaws who had gotten their comeuppance from the muzzle of his rifle. Slade spared them a glance, then asked, "Anybody hurt?"

One of the deputies, swearing wholeheartedly, was swabbing at a bullet-creased cheek. The sheriff was examining a slight gash along the back of his hand. Neither wound was of any consequence, Slade concluded. However, he thought it best to care for them. He turned and whistled a loud, clear note. A moment or two and Shadow came crashing through the brush, snorting inquiringly. Slade procured a jar of antiseptic salve and a roll of bandage and another of court plaster from his saddle pouches, with which he soon had the trifling injuries padded to halt the bleeding.

"Nothing to bother about," said the deputy with the creased cheek. "Scar will make me even purtier than I am now. But when I think of what would have happened if it hadn't been for you, Walt, I get the shakes." He mopped at his suddenly sweating face.

"Yes, we would have been sitting quail had we ridden up to the bodies," Slade conceded.

"You think of everything," snorted the sheriff.

"I had a somewhat similar experience once before," the Ranger replied. "Taught me to be careful and not take chances."

"Thank the blinkin' blue blazes you didn't take one this time," Medford said. "Suppose we look over the carcasses."

The two latest acquisitions of bodies revealed nothing other than the trinkets usually carried by range riders, and a surprisingly large sum of money, which the sheriff confiscated for the county treasury. As an afterthought, he handed each deputy twenty dollars.

"Guess you've earned it, and besides the rumhole dealers can use it. You, Wedburn, might see the doctor."

"Doctor, heck!" retorted the deputy, in injured tones. "I aim to see a bartender."

The remains of the drygulchers of the day before produced only empty pockets.

"Blasted ghouls!" growled Medford. "Even robbed the dead. Okay, boys, go fetch those dadblamed mules — guess they'll have to pack double. The blankety-blanks have it coming, especially the one who let out that beller. Otherwise we wouldn't have got nicked and might have been able to corral those two varmints while they were still in condition to talk."

The deputies hurried off to perform the chore. Medford scowled at the bodies. "Mean lookin' cusses, ain't they?" he remarked. "No, never saw them before, nor did the boys. What do you think?"

"About average, though somewhat above average in intelligence," Slade answered. "A snake-blooded outfit, all right. The devils intended plain murder, nothing less."

"And if it wasn't for you we'd walked into that trap — I'd just rather hear no more about it, I got the shakes, too," declared the sheriff. "You and your hunches, as you call 'em! Thank Pete you get 'em. Yes, the sidewinders figured to do for all of us. We'd sure have been nice targets when we unforked to look over the carcasses."

"Another example of rule by fear," Slade observed. "Folks are already a mite nervous where Loco Lobo is concerned. The murder of the sheriff of the county and his deputies would have had considerable effect and, among other things, tightened the latigos on jaws."

Medford shivered. "Say! I *don't* want to hear any more about it," he repeated. "Here come the boys with the mules; let's get outa here."

Slade was watchful during the ride to town, although he did not really anticipate further trouble. The sheriff and the deputies were nervous and ill at ease and heaved sighs of relief when they reached the cultivated lands and the ominous brush country was left behind. Farmers working the fields paused to stare as they passed but asked no questions.

It was different in Laredo. As the grim cortege threaded its way through the streets to the sheriff's office, a chattering crowd followed to fill the office, exclaiming, questioning, peering at the dead faces.

"A fine chore! A fine chore!" exclaimed one prominent citizen. "You are to be congratulated, Mr. Slade, and you, too, Sheriff. Looks like Loco Lobo is short a few. Fine! Fine!" And an old Mexican observed, "Ha! Now that *El Halcón* is here, all will indeed be well."

There were nods of agreement, but some among the gathering looked a trifle askance at the tall Ranger, and with puzzled expressions.

Owing to his habit of working alone and, whenever possible, undercover, often not revealing his Ranger connections, Walt Slade had built up a peculiar dual reputation. Those who knew the truth declared he was not only the most fearless but the ablest of the Rangers, while others who knew him only as *El Halcón* with killings to his credit, were wont to insist as vigorously that he was a blasted owlhoot too smart to get caught, so far. Private citizens were not supposed to take the law in their own hands, that was a chore for the duly elected or appointed law-enforcement officers.

However, Slade had champions as well as detractors who knew him only as *El Halcón*, who were wont to vow vehemently that he never killed anybody who didn't already have a killing overdue, that he was a credit to any community and that the "duly elected or appointed law-enforcement officers" were darn glad to have *El Halcón* lend a hand when the going got rough.

And the Mexican *peones* and other humble folk would say, "*El Halcón,* the just, the good, the compassionate, the friend of the lowly. *El Dios,* guard him!"

Slade knew well that the deception laid

him open to grave personal danger, but to that he gave little thought. It worried Captain Jim McNelty, the famous Commander of the Border Battalion of the Texas Rangers, who feared his Lieutenant and ace-man might come to harm at the hands of some mistaken deputy or marshal, to say nothing of some professional gun slinger out to enhance his reputation by downing the notorious *El Halcón* and not above shooting in the back to achieve his aims. But he admitted that as *El Halcón* of dubious reputation, Slade was able to learn things through avenues of information that would be closed to a known Ranger and that owlhoots, thinking him one of their own brand, would take chances they wouldn't take with a Ranger, to their undoing.

The prominent citizen, high in office in the town government, listened intently to the sheriff's version of the downing of the four outlaws, which stressed the part Slade played.

"The singingest man in the whole Southwest, with the fastest gunhand, that's what they call him," he remarked. "Well, I heard him sing once. I'd say, right on both counts." He shook hands with Slade.

So far, nobody was able to identify the four dead outlaws, or if they were, they refrained from saying so, not particularly to Slade's surprise. Folks might well be a bit reluctant when it came to sounding off about anybody suspected of being aligned with the terrible Loco Lobo.

"Maybe we'll have better luck when the boys from down around the riverfront and perhaps from Nuevo Laredo drop in," the sheriff predicted optimistically. "That's where the hellions would most likely hang out if they did come to town, and those barkeeps and other gents who hole up down there don't scare easy; to them Loco Lobo is just another hombre with the forked end down and a hat on top."

With which Slade was inclined to agree. The denizens of those dubious places of "entertainment" lived for the moment and gave scant thought to the future.

The crowd was dwindling. Medford shooed out the final stragglers and shut the door. "We've learned all we're going to, nothing at all, for the time being," he said. "Suppose we amble over to the Montezuma for a mite of a surrounding; I'm beginning to feel empty. Be dark 'fore long."

Slade was agreeable to the suggestion, so they locked the door and departed. The Montezuma was crowded, and, as was to be expected, others wished to hear about the day's happenings. After a while, however, Slade and the sheriff found a table and were permitted to enjoy their meal in peace.

"Guess we can't blame folks for getting worked up and curious," the sheriff observed. "They're sure for certain those hellions were some of Loco Lobo's bunch, and this is the first time any of the devils have been brought in. Of course people remember what you did to the Land Committee and those scalawags who tried to take over the irrigation project, but this business hits closer to home. With that sidewinder maverickin' all around, nobody feels safe. Everybody figures he may be next. We've had some bad ones hereabout, like El Cascabel, the Mexican bandit leader you cleaned up, for instance, but this one 'pears to be just about the worst ever. I still get the creeps when I think of that trap he laid for us."

"Yes, he's bad," Slade agreed. "Utterly ruthless, and appears to be shrewd, the sort hard to deal with. Looks like we have our work cut out for us."

"Well, as I've said before, my money's on *El Halcón*," the sheriff replied cheerfully. "Say, the news of what happened has sure livened the joint. Everybody happy, jabbering away a mile a minute, downing their

38

drinks as fast as the barkeeps can pour 'em. A real celebration."

"I fear their celebration is a mite premature," Slade said. "We managed to do for a few hired hands and that's all. Until we corral Loco Lobo himself, the chore isn't even started."

"Well," answered the sheriff, "as I've said before, my money's on *El Halcón*."

"Here's hoping you're picking a winner," Slade smiled.

4

There was no doubt but that the Montezuma was hopping, Slade was forced to admit. The roulette wheels whirred so fast they smoked. There was laughter and song, or something intended for it, at the crowded bar. The dance-floor girls were gay and animated and the orchestra appeared to have caught the prevailing excitement and fiddled and strummed away madly; and if a wrong note was sounded now and then, nobody noticed or cared. Altogether, very much like a cowhand payday celebration, with the clang of gold pieces on the "mahogany," and the sprightly click of bottle necks on glass rims to provide a fitting undertone to the general hullabaloo.

Slade studied the various patrons. There were cowhands, irrigation workers, business people from town, bearded farmers from the cultivated lands, and quite a few somewhat nondescript gentlemen who talked less and herded together more, and who appeared to be constantly surveying the reflections in the back bar mirror, their heads turning toward where conversations were in progress.

These interested *El Halcón,* being typical of the brand always infesting a boom town, on the lookout for opportunities of one sort or another. And Laredo was a boom town, with the great irrigation project going full blast and people of all kinds flocking into the valley from all over. The other valley towns were also affected, but Laredo was the focus. Suddenly he turned to Medford.

"As I understand it, your Loco Lobo, as you call him, pulled the Jimson store robbery lone-handed, right?"

"That's right," agreed the sheriff.

"And I suppose those two policemen you mentioned, who threw some lead at him, got a good look at him?"

"Right again," nodded the sheriff. "And so did some folks across the street. Oh, it was Loco Lobo, all right. Why?"

Slade did not immediately answer the question, and countered with one of his own: "And when he robbed the Zapata bank, I recall you saying that a clerk was hid in a back room and got a look at what happened, and at Loco Lobo and reported

41

it. And Lobo was not masked. How about those with him, they were masked, were they not?"

"By gosh! Come to think about it, the clerk said they were, but Loco Lobo, who was giving the orders, wasn't. How in blazes did you figure that out?" asked Medford.

Slade smiled slightly. "And his description of Lobo was a tall man with a very dark complexion and a very prominent nose. With flaring nostrils?"

"Guess that's right, too," Medford admitted, looking mystified. "Walt, what the devil are you getting at, anyhow?"

"Just this," Slade replied. "That clerk would never have stayed *hidden* in the back room, and alive, had not Lobo wished him to remain 'hidden' and see all that went on, including a good look at himself. Just as in the case of the Jimson robbery he gave quite a few folks a chance to get a good look at him."

"But he took a heck of a chance, holding up that store lone-handed," protested Medford.

"Yes, he did," Slade agreed, "but there are some men who know fear only from the murky conception they get from a dictionary definition, if they have ever happened to look into a dictionary, and evidently Loco

42

Lobo is one of them. As to his reason for letting folks get a look at him, including that clerk, who otherwise would have been slaughtered along with the cashier, and the other clerk, he wished them to 'see' Loco Lobo as they did see him. Now everybody is on the lookout for a big tall jigger with a very dark complexion and an unusually prominent nose."

"But what in blazes does that get him?" demanded the bewildered sheriff. "If he shows up in town, somebody will spot him, sure as the devil; that sort of a face sticks in the memory."

"Exactly," Slade smiled. "It does. First we will take the complexion angle. There are any number of preparations, including some remarkable ones employed by various Indian tribes in the course of tribal ceremonials, that will darken the complexion in a manner to defy detection. Water won't affect them, but plenty of soap, or soap weed where the Indians were concerned, washes it off easily."

"Okay," said the sheriff. "But how about the hellion's nose? Couldn't wash that off."

"Hardly," Slade agreed. "But changing a nose is quite a simple matter. Cotton plugs, properly prepared and deftly inserted in the nostrils will greatly broaden a nose at the base and cause the nostrils to flare. The clerk mentioned that Lobo's lip drew up from his teeth; fairly good evidence that he was breathing through his mouth instead of his nose, and not accustomed to doing so."

"Is there anything you miss!" the sheriff moaned despairingly.

"Plenty," Slade admitted with a smile. "But such a thing as we are discussing is quite obvious to any observant person." Medford snorted explosively and waited for more.

"And, in addition, a skillful application of wax can build up the bridge. So quickly you have a nose radically different than the one nature provided," Slade concluded his summary. "Both complexion and nose are out of the ordinary, and it is something out of the ordinary that most folks note and remember. Your Loco Lobo may very well be a man of florid or bronzed complexion, with an insignificant nose and possibly blond or tawny hair when it is not dyed. As such, he may be sitting at the table behind you and you wouldn't realize it."

The sheriff glanced hastily over his shoulder, looked sheepish, and grinned.

"So it 'pears we're up against something a mite out of the ordinary," he commented.

"Yes," Slade conceded. "A cold killer with

brains; the very worst type of criminal. Running him down is likely to pose something of a chore. Well, we'll see."

Medford ordered another snort, over which he muttered and grumbled. Slade resumed his study of faces. Among those "uncertain" individuals at the bar or lounging about the room might very well be, he knew, one or more of Loco Lobo's bunch looking things over, picking up stray bits of information that might provide something lucrative. Or they might have an even more sinister activity in mind, especially where he himself was concerned.

So while he appeared to be thoroughly at ease, in reality he was very much on the alert, missing no move at the bar or elsewhere in the room, noting and evaluating every man who pushed through the swinging doors. For he knew he was playing a lethal game of wits with a cunning and utterly unscrupulous character — with death very probably the forfeit for a mistake.

Just the same he was forced to admit he enjoyed such a contest, and had no doubt as to the ultimate outcome — which was perhaps the foremost secret of Walt Slade's outstanding success as a Texas Ranger: he believed in himself.

Well, at least it appeared that this time he

wouldn't find himself mixed up in a complex tangle of shady business manipulations engineered by evasive miscreants as bad as any outlaw that ever rode the brush.

"Engineered" caused him to lapse for the moment into restrospect, reviewing the series of events that were responsible for him being a Texas Ranger instead of something radically different.

Shortly before the death of his father, which followed business reverses that cost the elder Slade his ranch, young Walt had graduated from an outstanding college of engineering. He had planned to take a postgraduate course in special subjects to better fit him for the profession he had determined to make his life work. This, however, became impossible for the time being and he was undecided as to just what his next move should be when he happened to pay a visit to Ranger Captain Jim Mc-Nelty. Captain Jim had a suggestion to make.

"Walt," he said, "why not come into the Rangers for a while? You'd have plenty of spare time in which to pursue your studies. You seemed to like the work when you served with me some during summer vacations. What do you say?"

After a short period of reflection, Slade

concluded the idea wasn't bad, and decided to give it a whirl. He did like Ranger work. And there was the catch. As he went along, he liked it more and more, for it provided so many opportunities of righting wrongs, helping deserving people, and making the great land he loved an even better place for the decent and law abiding. And he found himself loath to sever connections with the illustrious body of law-enforcement officers, even though, having long since gotten more from private study than he could have hoped for from the postgrad, he had received lucrative offers of employment from such outstanding giants of the business world as Jaggers Dunn, General Manager of the C. & P. Railroad System; former Governor of Texas, Jim Hogg; and that fabulous Wall Street tycoon, John Warne "Bet-a-Million" Gates. He was young — plenty of time to be an engineer. He'd stick with the Rangers for a while.

5

Abruptly Slade was snapped out of his reverie by the appearance of a lithe young Mexican who pushed through the swinging doors and glanced about expectantly. It was Pancho Garza, one of Miguel Sandoval's "young men," as he called certain individuals who helped keep order in his place, in whose company Slade had experienced stirring adventures in the course of his former visits to Laredo.

Spotting Slade and the sheriff in that swift, all-embracing glance, Pancho sauntered to the table and accepted a chair and a drink. Knowing he had information to impart, Slade waited.

Pancho downed his drink as if the fiery liquor were so much water and spoke, his lips moving not at all.

"Capitan," he asked, "seek you the *ladrone El Lobo Loco?"*

Slade nodded.

"So I assumed," Pancho said in his precise Mission-taught English. "*Capitan,* he is here."

"Here, in Laredo?"

"That is right. At a place on Zarazoga Street near San Agustin Avenue, a place you will recall is owned by an *amigo* of mine, an *Americano.*"

Slade remembered the place, which had a reputation for catering to a rough element, but was run on the square.

"Pancho, are you sure?" he asked.

"I am sure," the Mexican replied positively. "It is he. My *amigo* knows. He and four others, men most evil."

"Walt," the sheriff broke in excitedly, "it looks like this is our chance to drop a loop on the sidewinder."

"Perhaps," the Ranger answered. Privately he thought the thing appeared just a mite too simple, and he suffered an uneasy presentiment that somehow a trap was set.

"Five," he remarked musingly. "Well, I've a notion the three of us can handle them, if it comes to a showdown."

"*Capitan,* I can promise you one, perhaps two," Pancho said cheerfully, caressing the haft of his long knife. Slade knew a second blade nestled in the top of his boot. He

49

waited until the Mexican had downed another drink, then said, "All right, let's go. By way of Flores Avenue, Pancho, and stop at the corner of Zarazoga."

They sauntered from the saloon. A few steps and Slade called a halt. For several moments he gazed back at the door of the Montezuma; nobody came out.

"Looks like we're not wearing a tail," he said and continued to Flores Avenue, then turned south.

Before long, the damp smell of the river struck their nostrils. Ahead and slightly to the right, the spidery outlines of the International Bridge at the foot of Convent Avenue loomed against the sky. They walked on, slowly, Slade setting the pace, his eyes constantly scanning the terrain ahead. When they reached Zarazoga Street he paused and peered around the corner.

The street was deserted. Near the corner of San Agustin Avenue he could make out the glow of the saloon's dingy window.

"Pancho," he asked, "isn't there an alley in back of the saloon?"

"*Si,*" Pancho replied.

"And a back door opening onto the alley?"

Pancho grinned wolfishly, getting the drift. "There is," he said.

"Think we could get in by way of that back door?"

"We can, I have a key," Pancho answered. "My *amigo* trusts me."

Slade nodded, studied the lighted window a moment longer. "Okay," he said, "I think it's safe to cross the street. Make it snappy."

They raced across the street with nothing happening. There was no street between Zarazoga and the river, but there was a jumble of unlighted shacks and a warehouse or two. Between these they threaded their way and reached the back door in question. Pancho inserted a key in the lock. The bolt slid back without a sound and he cautiously opened the door to reveal a dimly lighted and unoccupied back room. Facing them was a second door that led to the saloon. They glided to it. Pancho slowly turned the knob, opened the door a crack and peered through.

"The four at the far end of the bar," he breathed. "They look toward the swinging doors and wait. *El Lobo Loco* I do not see."

Slade hesitated. With Loco Lobo not in their company, they had absolutely nothing on the four killers whose intent watch on the swinging doors evinced their intention — nothing which would justify arresting them. He decided boldness would be the

51

best course.

"Fan out and be ready for business," he whispered to his companions. He flung open the door, kicked over a nearby chair that fell with a clatter. The four men turned in the direction of the noise, stared. One gave an alarmed yelp —

"Look out! It's him!" Hands streaked to holsters.

Slade drew and shot with both hands. One of the quartette fell to lie motionless. Answering bullets thudded into the wall but none found a mark, for the outlaws, caught off balance, shot wildly. Pancho's long knife buzzed through the air like an angry hornet and ripped a second's throat wide open. The sheriff's gun boomed and a third went down. The one remaining on his feet whirled and fled madly for the swinging doors. Slade tried to line sights with him, but now men scattering wildly from the bar were between him and the target and he was forced to hold his fire. Pancho tried with his other knife, throwing down with a spiraling movement, but the blade thudded into the door an instant too late. The fugitive was already through. Attempting pursuit would be just a waste of time.

The place was in an uproar — men yelling, dance-floor girls shrieking, overturned chairs and tables clattering. Slade's great voice rolled in thunder through the room —

"Hold it! Everything's under control! Quiet down so we can hear ourselves think!"

The tumult stilled a little; something like order was restored. The burly owner came hurrying forward, a sawed-off shotgun in his hand, a grin splitting his rugged face.

"Good work, Mr. Slade! Good work, Sheriff!" he exclaimed. "Was all set to lend a hand but things happened so fast I didn't get a chance." He waved the cocked sawed-off in a manner that caused some frantic ducking to get out of line.

"Oh, they were some of Loco Lobo's bunch," he replied to Slade's question. "I recognized the big-nosed hellion right off, and so did a couple of the boys; nothing we could do about it except try to get word to you. Reckon Pancho did, eh? Lobo himself slipped out just a little after Pancho left, leaving those four vinegaroons watching the door. He was here only a minute or two."

"And I suppose Pancho left by way of the back room?" Slade said.

"I did," Pancho broke in. "I thought it best."

"Might have been, except Lobo watched you leave and knew you were on your way to me and the sheriff," Slade said. "That's what he planned you or somebody to do."

"And if it wasn't for you, we would have barged in the front way and got blowed from under our hats," said the sheriff. "Carter, he never misses a bet."

"Guess he don't," agreed Carter, the owner. "Well, here comes the police chief and a couple of his pavement pounders, late as usual. Hello, Chief, how about one on the house?"

"Don't mind if I do," replied the plump and jolly chief, twinkling his shrewd little eyes at Slade, who remembered him well. "Somebody said you were having a mite of trouble down here. Why don't you move those carcasses out of the door before somebody gets hurt? I nearly fell over them. Want to get sued?"

"Ain't my game," Carter returned cheerfully. "I never meddle with what another fellow's bagged."

However, he ordered a couple of swampers to drag the bodies out of the way.

"I'll have some of the boys rustle a shutter or two and pack them to your office, Tobe," he offered. "Suppose old Doc Cooper, the coroner, will want to hold an inquest."

"Much obliged," accepted the sheriff. "Yes, we're getting quite a collection for Doc to set on."

Slade turned to the young Mexican. "Pancho, slip over to Miguel's place and tell them there that everything is okay," he requested. "Chances are they've heard something and may be worried. And thank you for everything."

"I fear I very nearly led *Capitan* into trouble," Pancho replied gloomily. "But I thought I was acting for the best."

"You did fine," Slade assured him. "Things worked out very much to our advantage."

"*Si,* thanks to *El Halcón* who sees all and knows all," Pancho said, and headed for Miguel's cantina.

Word of the ruckus had gotten around and now the place was packed. Slade, studying expressions, shrewdly suspected that among those who viewed the bodies were some who recalled seeing the three outlaws in life but refrained from coming forward. At least in public. Perhaps somebody would later appear with a little confidential information. He hoped so, but was not overly optimistic.

The shutters were procured, the bodies loaded onto them. The police chief accompanied Slade and the sheriff to the office and the details of the incident were reviewed for his benefit. He shook hands with Slade again.

"I don't know what we'd do without you," he declared. "This town is sure deeply in your debt. Sheriff, why don't you persuade him to take up permanent residence here?"

"Oh, he's got itchy feet and can't keep still," Medford replied. "Maybe he'll quiet down after a while; a good reason why he should stay here."

"You're right," agreed the chief. "She's a darn nice gal."

They acquired quite a following on the way to the office. The bodies were examined, but with negative results so far as any recalling anything concerning them. Finally Medford showed everybody out and closed and locked the door.

"The nerve of that sidewinder," he growled, apropos of Loco Lobo. "Sashaying into town that way where anybody could see him."

"Which was exactly what he wished — to be seen," Slade said. "Stayed just long enough for folks in Carter's place to get a look at him and recognize him as the notorious Loco Lobo. Watched Pancho slip out the back way and then high-tailed, leaving his men to handle the chore. Very smooth, but just a mite too obvious."

"For you, I suppose," the sheriff agreed

wearily. "I would have fallen for it, and so would have most anybody else. How you figure things out as you do is beyond me."

"It really was obvious," Slade repeated. "I am convinced that Lobo wears a disguise. In a way, he contradicts the usual purpose of a disguise, which as a rule is to render the wearer unrecognizable and not conspicuous. Like a man who is usually clean shaven and grows a beard, perhaps darkens it and his hair, easy enough if you know how. His appearance is ordinary and folks pay him little mind. Lobo wishes to attract attention, wishes folks to remember his appearance, which is out of the ordinary. It works, to a degree, at least. So when he barged into Carter's place as he did, why? Shrewd and far-seeing, he knew perfectly well that somebody would take the word to you, and to me, seeing as I was known to be in your company. So, not unnaturally, I wondered just why he should do what he did and, I repeat, the answer was quite obvious. Where he made a bad slip was in the course of the robbery at the Zapata bank."

"How's that?" Medford asked.

"He had his followers masked, while he was not," Slade explained. "So the clerk who escaped being murdered with the others, gave an excellent description of his appearance, which coincided with that provided by others who had gotten a look at Loco Lobo. So everybody was on the lookout for dark-faced, big-nosed Loco Lobo, while, as I mentioned before, Loco Lobo without his disguise could show up anywhere, mingle with any crowd, and not be noticed. Beginning to understand?"

"Oh, sure!" snorted the sheriff. "All plumb plain, now, but why didn't somebody else think of it? Why didn't I think of it?"

Slade smiled and did not attempt to answer. "What we've got to think on and think on hard," he observed, "is where will the devil strike next. He will, and soon, you can rely on that. Could we anticipate what he has in mind and get the jump on him, we might be able to eradicate the pest for once and all."

They discussed various possibilities but with no satisfactory results. Loco Lobo had a wide area for his operations and trying to pin down his probable move was like trying to pick a flea off a hot skillet.

Finally Slade said, "Suppose we give those bodies a once-over. Might hit on something of interest. Not likely, though; that sort seldom packs anything worth while."

The pockets of the dead men divulged nothing he considered significant save quite a bit of money until the sheriff drew a folded sheet of paper from a shirt pocket.

"What's this?" he wondered. "All sorts of funny looking lines penciled on it." He turned it upside down, sideways, righted it and shook his head. "Looks like some sort of a puzzle," he said, passing the sheet to Slade.

The Ranger received it, glanced over it. Refolding it, he stowed it in one of his own pockets.

"Keep it for a souvenir," he announced. Medford shot him a quick glance, but refrained from asking questions he knew very well would not be answered.

Slade turned his attention back to the bodies, scrutinizing the dead features with care, giving particular heed to the man whose pocket had discovered the slip of paper. He rocked back on his heels, still regarding that individual, and spoke.

"A man much above the average in intelligence, I'd say," he remarked. "Intelligent and capable. Quite likely Lobo's chief lieutenant, his second in command, entrusted with the more difficult chores in the absence of the chief. I think he was the only one of the four in the saloon who was not completely flabbergasted by the surprise we gave them. He was the only one who was deliberately lining sights when Pancho's knife got him in the throat. If Pancho wasn't greased lightning and uncannily accurate in his handling of a blade, he might very well have done for one of us."

"You figure he might be the brains of the outfit?" Medford asked.

Slade shook his head. "No, I don't think so," he replied. "I still figure Lobo does his own thinking and planning and directs the raids, although he may not always be present. But I am of the opinion that this fellow carried out orders and often did the field work.

"That," he added, tapping his pocket, "is why I am inclined to attach significance to the drawing he was carrying; a chance it might really mean something. What? At the moment I haven't the slightest idea, but I intend to give the matter some serious thought."

Finally, he carefully examined the dead hands, and after doing so, gestured to the individual under discussion.

"The others," he said, "have undoubtedly at one time or another been cowhands, a couple of them quite recently, I would say. But if this fellow ever was, it was a long, long time ago. I seem to discern slightly, hardly visible scars of rope and branding iron, but I'd hesitate to say for sure."

"Well, if you can't see 'em, I'd say they ain't there," declared Medford.

"Perhaps," Slade conceded. "Anyhow, the hellion interests me, and he may, in retrospect, prove the weak link in Loco Lobo's chain. We'll see."

The sheriff straightened up and resumed his chair. "Now what?" he asked.

"I think I'll mosey down to Miguel's cantina," Slade replied.

"Watch your step," the sheriff cautioned. "The hellions might be out to even up the score."

"I doubt if they'll make another move tonight," Slade said. "What happened must have given them something of a jolt, and will take them a little time to recover."

Medford regarded the bodies with satisfaction. "One thing sure for certain, we're thinning 'em out," he remarked. "Seven ain't a bad bag, not bad at all."

"But until we drop a loop on Loco Lobo, we haven't accomplished much," Slade reminded him.

"Just a matter of time," Medford returned cheerfully. "Just a matter of time. Okay, be seeing you. I'm going to bed."

When Slade reached the cantina, Marie was on the floor. While waiting until she was free, he unfolded the sheet of paper taken from the dead outlaw's pocket and studied it intently. He had at once recognized the thing as a neatly drawn plat of the irrigation project to the east of Laredo. At one point a tiny "x" was inscribed. To all appearances it was a direction sheet drawn by somebody who was no slouch with a pencil and had an accurate eye for distance and direction.

What did it mean? He hadn't the slightest idea, but was determined to try and find out. So far as he knew, the project was beset with no difficulties at present. On the occasion of his former visit to the section, he had forced certain predatory interests to the wall and had frustrated a skillfully conceived plot by those interests to take over the project to the detriment of the settlers of the valley. Since then the project appeared to be going along smoothly and with speed. What the devil was in the wind?

It didn't seem reasonable to think that Loco Lobo who, so far as anybody knew, was just a brush-popping owlhoot with more brains than average, could be mixed up in something harmful to the project. But after all, Loco Lobo was undoubtedly an uncertain quantity and could well be something different from what he appeared.

Slade wondered if unexpected complications were due. With a shake of his head, he refolded the paper and stowed it in his pocket, the concentration furrow deepening between his black brows, a sure sign *El Halcón* was doing some thinking.

A little later, Marie joined him and regarded him accusingly.

"Same old story," she said. "Out of my sight a minute and you're in trouble. I thought you were on vacation."

"I thought so, too, but it doesn't seem to work out that way," he replied morosely.

"Oh, you don't mind," she retorted. "You're not happy unless you're living dangerously."

"You should know," he said, crinkling his eyes at her.

"Oh, I'm not so bad," she replied. "I just try to tighten the tie rope a little. Yes, Pancho told us all about it. Everybody is singing your praises. Including, of course, myself," she added, flashing her charming smile and fluttering her long lashes. "Oh, I'm proud of you all right, but you sure keep me in a constant state of tremulous anticipation."

Slade laughed. "Well, are you ever disappointed?"

Marie giggled and did not answer.

"Rosa and Estaban will be here shortly," she said. "They stopped to visit with friends first. I told them you would very likely be late, as usual. Here they come now!"

Rosa Fuentes was taller than Marie, but she had the same slender, graceful figure and beautiful eyes. Estaban, lean, wiry, with a dark, immobile countenance, was an excellent example of the best type of Spanish-Mexican. Both greeted Slade warmly and sat down. Rosa's eyes were filled with laughter.

"Doesn't Marie look radiant?" she said to Slade. "Looks just like a bride, a bride of a couple of years, of course."

"Rosa!" Marie exclaimed, blushing hotly, "you are impossible."

"Why?" Rosa asked, all innocence. "What's wrong with looking like a bride? I looked like one myself once, years ago."

"I don't think you've changed much, eh, Estaban?" Slade smiled.

"Just a little bossier," replied Estaban. "Can't call my life my own. She made me change my shirt before coming to town, and I'd only worn it a month."

"That's a deliberate falsehood," declared Rosa. "I scrub my fingers to the bone keeping you clean."

Glancing at the slender, almond-nailed

digits in question, Slade felt they hadn't suffered much.

Miguel joined them, bottles under his arm. He bowed over Rosa's hand, although his body was not formed to bend that way, and filled glasses to the brim.

"A day of gladness," he said, raising his own.

"I'm hungry, and so is Estaban, and Marie always is," said Rosa.

"The food is prepared," replied the genial host. "Miguel anticipates."

They had a very pleasant dinner together and talked over incidents of Slade's previous visits. He had several dances with both girls and felt the hectic day and night hadn't worked out too bad, after all. With the dawn not far off, they walked under the stars to the little house with the garden and the flowers.

The following afternoon, Slade saddled up and rode east on Matamoros Street, heading for the present site of the irrigation project. Shadow splashed through the shallow water of Zacate Creek and they continued on their way.

Slade rode slowly, enjoying the green and gold beauty of the day. He experienced a quiet satisfaction as he viewed the scene of prosperity spread before his eyes. Already great progress had been made during the year that had passed since his previous visit to the project. What had been square miles of semiarid terrain was now fertile farming land, with springing crops, little homes, and happy people. Progress! Man battling the imponderable, ofttimes savage forces of Nature, and winning. He was uplifted by the remembrance that he had played a part in this great development.

Finally he reached the area of operations, a scene of bustling activity and orderly confusion. Here pile drivers thudded, air compressors chattered, steam shovels gouged out great mouthfuls of earth, picks and shovels flashed back the sun, irrigation ditches sparkled. He paused a moment to watch a ponderous "hydraulic giant" battering down banks of gravel preparatory to the construction of an impounding basin.

The giant, with a nozzle with a double joint that could be turned in a horizontal or a vertical plane, sent forth a hissing stream of water under high pressure provided by a big air compressor that was directed against the bank. Such a giant spouted fifty cubic feet of water per second at a velocity of a hundred and eighty feet per second. Under the terrific beat of the steel-hard jet, the packed gravel dissolved like sugar — fast and efficient. The project employed the most modern machinery. He rode on, viewing the various activities and finally located Ernest Clark, the engineer in charge, who was beholden to him for invaluable assistance in the course of the Ranger's former contacts with the project.

Clark greeted him effusively and led the way to a cook shanty for coffee and a snack, and a surrounding of oats for Shadow, who remembered him well as a dispenser of delectable provender.

While they ate, they discussed matters relative to the project. Clark was enthusiastic.

"Yes, we're rolling toward San Ygnacio," he said. "Everything going like clockwork, thanks largely to what you accomplished here for us last year. No difficulties that pose serious problems. The boys are sort of hopping today and making the dirt fly in anticipation for their payday bust. Tomorrow is payday and they get the day off. Laredo will howl tomorrow and tomorrow night."

"Pay off in cash?" Slade asked casually.

"That's right," replied Clark. "The boys like it better that way. We'll start paying early for the money's already in the office safe over there." He gestured out the window to a squat building set somewhat apart and quite a distance from the big barracks that housed the workers.

"Guarded, of course, although we've had no trouble that way," he added. Slade nodded and closed his eyes a moment; he was reviewing the directional lines on the slip of paper in his pocket. Unless he was greatly mistaken, and he didn't believe he was, the tiny "x" on the slip definitely located the office building in question.

They talked a while longer, over more coffee. Then Slade announced his intention of returning to Laredo.

"Come again soon," begged Clark. "Nice to have you, and every now and then some little matter comes up on which I'd appreciate your advice."

"I'll be back very shortly," *El Halcón* replied with a significance that was lost on the engineer. He was very thoughtful as he rode to town, the concentration furrow deep between his black brows.

"Horse," he said to Shadow, "I'm going to play a hunch. May be a loco one, but somehow I don't think it is. Especially when it concerns a gent called 'Loco.' If it doesn't pan out, nothing's lost except a little time, and your legs need a mite of stretching anyhow." Shadow snorted and did not commit himself, although he did roll a somewhat dubious eye at his master, as if to say that loco might apply elsewhere. Slade chuckled and rode on toward the rose and scarlet splendor of the sunset, arriving at Laredo as the impalpable blue dust of the dusk was sifting its old but ever new enchantment over the rangeland and the farms.

After stabling his horse, he headed for the Montezuma, knowing it was about time for Sheriff Medford to be partaking of his evening surrounding.

His surmise proved correct. He found the old peace officer comfortably ensconced at a table with a full plate in front of him, plying a busy knife and fork. Slade joined him in a bite.

After a while, Medford pushed back his plate, ordered a snort and shot the Ranger an interrogative glance.

"Was down at the irrigation project looking things over," Slade replied to the unspoken question. "They're making fine progress."

"Yes, they are," the sheriff agreed. "And tomorrow the workers will be making 'progress' of a different sort — their payday. A rough and ready bunch, but not bad. A busted nose or two and a few skinned heads about all. Very few of them ever pack a gun. Just free spenders out for a good time. Have to keep an eye on them down around the river joints, to make sure some sharpies don't put something over on them. What's on your mind?"

"Nothing much," Slade answered carelessly. "Think I'll take another little ride after a bit." The sheriff looked suspicious.

"Hanker for company?" he asked pointedly. Slade shook his head.

"Just aim to do a little exploring," he said. "It's a nice night."

Medford did not appear convinced but evidently decided to let it go at that.

"I'm ambling out for a look-see, after I finish my snort," he said. "Things 'pear quiet enough, but you never can tell of late. By the way, the coroner holds an inquest at two 'clock tomorrow. Be nice if we had a few more specimens for him to set on."

"Yes, it would," Slade smiled. "Perhaps you'll be able to accommodate." Medford snorted.

"More likely you will," he said. "You and your rides! Okay, see you later." He moseyed out. Slade sat sipping coffee and smoking for another hour. Then, glancing at the clock, he too departed and headed for Shadow's stable.

70

"Here we go again, horse," he said. "And if my hunch proves to be a straight one, there may be a mite more work for old Doc tomorrow. Of one sort or another," he added grimly. "We're going up against a hard man who doesn't miss many bets. That is, if we're not riding a cold trail and something really develops."

It was a nice night, at first, with the stars glowing golden in the vast, blue-black sweep of the heavens, but as he rode on at a good pace, a film of cloud crept across the sky, dimming the starlight, and the night became very dark.

"May work to our advantage, though," he told the horse. "Hope so."

He had declined the sheriff's offer of company for two reasons. First, he was confident that with the element of surprise in his favor, he could handle any situation that might develop alone, and he did not wish to subject the sturdy old law-enforcement officer to needless danger. Secondly, he reasoned that one was less liable to detection by being overheard or otherwise than two. He himself could move like an Indian on even the darkest night, while the sheriff was not quite so adroit.

6

The miles flowed back under Shadow's speeding irons. No sound broke the great hush save the gurgling of the Rio Grande, not far off, the occasional call of a night bird and the distant yelping of some coyotes.

As he neared the site of the operation, Slade turned north until he reached a straggle of thicket, not far from the camp, he had noted earlier in the day. Slowing the pace, he rode in its shadow. Finally he drew rein and looked over the ground.

The big camp was dark and silent. Evidently the tired workers had gone to bed early to build up strength for the payday bust in the offing. Almost directly opposite where he sat his horse was the office building Clark had pointed out. In it a dim light burned, probably for the accommodation of the payroll money guard.

After a moment of contemplating, Slade

unforked and dropped the split reins to the ground.

"Stay put," he whispered to Shadow and stole forward on foot, hoping the guard, if he was on the job, wouldn't take a shot at him.

Step by slow step he moved toward the building. Soon he was very close. His caution redoubled. Then abruptly he gave voice to an exasperated mutter. Under a nearby tree he could just make out the shadowy outlines of three horses. Looked like he had miscalculated and was a mite late. He quickened his pace, for now he greatly feared he need pay the unfortunate guard no mind.

With a quick, light tread he sped toward the building. It boasted a little covered porch, and under the porch was a door that stood nearly half open. Noiselessly, with infinite caution, he mounted the two steps to the porch and eased forward. Now, peering around the edge of the door, he could see that a bracket lamp, turned very low, was secured to the far wall, showing the dark opening of a second door that probably led to an inner room. Near the door stood a big iron safe, the beam of a dark lantern trained on its face, beside which squatted three men. A faint whining sound broke the silence. His hunch was a straight one!

Guns ready for instant action, he eased forward another step, into the room, opened his lips to call, "Up! You're covered!"

But before he could speak, his forward reaching foot came down on a loose board that creaked loudly.

The three men leaped to their feet, whirled around. Slade got a glimpse of a dark countenance, a great beak of a nose, and blazing eyes. A hand flickered like the beat of a falcon's wing.

Slade went sideways along the wall, but not quite fast enough. Lights blazed before his eyes. Bell notes stormed in his ears. Half blinded by the bullet that grazed his temple, he poured lead across the room as fast as he could pull trigger. He heard a gasping cry, a thud, a patter of fast steps, the bang of a door slammed open. Still groggy, he floundered across to the inner room. To his ears, now clearing, came the thud of fast hoofs fading into the distance. Shaking his head to free his brain of cobwebs, he turned back.

On the floor in front of the safe lay a motionless form. Slade glanced at the contorted face and swore a bitter oath. It was not the man with the dark complexion and the big nose. Loco Lobo had escaped!

His head still throbbing, Slade leaned against the door jamb for a moment, breathing deeply. Now the camp was in an uproar, shouting, cursing men pouring from the barracks in all stages of undress, some bearing lanterns, others pick handles for clubs. Slade stepped into view.

"Quiet!" he thundered at them. "Where's Mr. Clark?"

"It's Mr. Slade!" a voice shouted. "What happened, Mr. Slade? We'll fetch Mr. Clark."

"Scatter around and see if you can find the guard, or what's left of him," Slade directed.

"Here comes Mr. Clark," somebody whooped. "This way, Mr. Clark."

The engineer, shirtless and shoeless, came hurrying forward.

"Slade!" he exclaimed. "What in blazes?"

"Take a look," *El Halcón* replied, gesturing to the safe. Circling the combination knob were three overlapping holes. The bit of a hand drill that lay on the floor was stuck in a fourth hole.

"A few more minutes and they'd have had the safe open and cleaned," Slade said.

Clark swore explosively. "And you stopped them, eh?" he said.

"Sort of," the Ranger admitted.

At that moment a cry sounded in back of the building, "Here he is! Looks like he's a goner!"

"Come on," Slade told the engineer and led the way out the back door.

The guard lay on his face, his hat jammed down over his ears. Slade gently turned him over on his back and felt his heart.

"Still beating, and fairly strong," he announced. He pulled off the crushed hat to reveal a heavy stocking-cap worn under it, the night being cold.

"That's what saved him," Slade said as he removed the cap. "Otherwise the chances are his skull would have been shattered." With sensitive fingertips, he explored a big bruise on the side of the guard's head.

"No sign of fracture I can ascertain," he concluded. "May be concussion, however. All right, carry him inside and cover him up on a bunk. I'll give him another look shortly, and I'll send the doctor from town for a thorough examination."

"Say!" Clark suddenly exclaimed, "there's blood on *your* face; you're hurt."

"Nothing to bother about," Slade replied. "Slug barely broke the skin but gave me a nasty wallop. Otherwise I might have done a better chore on the devils. Yes, it was Loco

76

Lobo and a couple of his bunch. I got a glimpse of him as he turned, and he came very nearly doing a finish job on me."

"I'm completely bewildered," declared the engineer. "Come on and we'll get some hot coffee and you can sort of line me up."

"Just a minute," Slade answered. "I wish to see what the one I bagged has on him. Something another member of the bunch was packing saved your payroll money tonight."

Peering into the dead face, which was rather scrubby, he catalogued the fellow as an average brush-popping owlhoot with nothing outstanding about him. Nor did his pockets reveal anything of importance save a good deal of money, which Slade replaced.

The workers, still excited and talkative, were clustered in front of the building. Clark raised his hand to still the tumult.

"Back to bed, boys," he told them. "You'll have your payday bust — money's safe — but if it wasn't for Mr. Slade, there would have been slim pickin's tomorrow."

"Hurrah for Mr. Slade, he saved us from dyin' of thirst!" a voice shouted. The cheer that followed quivered the building.

The men trooped back to bed, Slade and the engineer following. As they neared the barracks, a man stuck his head out the door.

"Hutchins, the guard, has come out of it," he called. "Don't think he's hurt much, from the way he's cussin'."

Slade interviewed Hutchins, but learned nothing.

"Thought I heard a noise behind the shack, stuck my head out the back door and the sky fell in on me," he replied to the Ranger's question. "Nope, didn't see anybody. Didn't see anything but a lot of stars. Don't remember anything else. Think I can go to town with the rest of the boys?"

"I'd say you can, if you feel okay in the morning," Slade decided. "Better stop at the doctor's office, though, and let him look you over. Okay, Clark, let's get that coffee; I can use a snort of it about now."

Outside, Slade whistled to Shadow, who appeared shortly, snorting his disgust with things in general. He was somewhat appeased by a generous surrounding of oats.

Slade retrieved the dead outlaw's horse from where it was still tethered under the tree and stabled it. The brand it bore was, he believed, an East Texas burn, but he wasn't sure. Meant little anyhow, horses could be sold, bought, traded, or stolen and would often turn up a long distance from where they were foaled.

Over coffee and sandwiches, Slade filled

in the details of the affair for the engineer's benefit, and showed him the plat taken from the dead outlaw's pocket.

"Naturally I recognized the thing for what it was," he concluded. "And when I saw the little 'x' pinpointed the office building where the money was kept, I played a hunch that Lobo planned to make a try for it. I imagine the chore was delegated to the man who packed this thing, but his unexpected demise evidently caused Lobo to handle the business in person. Looks that way."

Clark shook his head in admiration. "Don't you ever miss a bet?" he marveled.

El Halcón smiled, a trifle wryly. "I very nearly missed one tonight, leaning against the hot end of a slug," he replied.

"You all right?" the engineer asked anxiously.

"Fit as a fiddle, it was just a scratch," Slade answered. "I'll put a little cold water on it and it'll be okay." He proceeded to do so.

"And now I'm heading to town," he said. "The night will be pretty well along by the time I get there. See you in the Montezuma tomorrow night perhaps."

With Shadow in good shape, Slade rode fast and it lacked several hours of dawn when he reached Laredo. After caring for his mount, he made his way to Miguel's cantina, feeling fairly sure that the sheriff would be awaiting him there.

He was. Marie shuddered and Medford swore under his breath as Slade recounted the night's adventure.

"The devil is lightning fast on the draw," he concluded apropos of Loco Lobo. "The moment I gave them to surrender very nearly proved my undoing."

"You shouldn't have done it," growled the sheriff. "You should have plugged the blankety-blanks — excuse me, Marie — when they stood up."

"Perhaps," Slade conceded, "but it is instinct with a Ranger to give the opportunity to surrender. Well, anyhow, there's the other specimen you wished for your inquest."

Marie insisted on plastering the slight cut at his temple despite his protests that it was nothing.

"Shut up!" she ordered. "If you haven't enough sense to take care of yourself, somebody has to do it for you."

Clark, the irrigation project engineer, obligingly packed the body of the dead outlaw into one of the big wagons that brought the workers to town for their bust. So all

80

specimens were present and accounted for when at two o'clock the coroner held a short and informal inquest. Old Doc had other things to do and directed a verdict that acquitted everybody and praised everybody. "Plant 'em and bring in some more!" The jury concurred. Court adjourned to the Montezuma for refreshment.

After which Slade and the sheriff went into executive session, discussing the situation as it stood and endeavoring to anticipate what would be Loco Lobo's next move.

"He'll be making one soon," the Ranger predicted. "Must have been somewhat shaken by recent happenings, and I'd say the loss of that payroll money he counted on hurt. He has to keep his men supplied with plenty of spending money or he'll have trouble with them. He's bad, all right, but the hellions who follow his lead aren't exactly lambs, and there's a limit to what they'll put up with from a leader who fails to produce results. The loss of more than a half dozen of his hands has likely got the rest sort of jumpy."

"They'll jump before *El Halcón* is finished with them," growled Medford. "Looks like he must be running a mite short of hands."

"Yes, but he can get more," Slade pointed out. "This is a fertile field for outlaws and always has been. We've got our work cut out for us."

"Won't be the first time," the sheriff observed cheerfully. "Everything will work out hunky-dory, as usual."

"If I'd just moved a little faster last night, we might not have to worry about the sidewinder," Slade remarked.

"Got a notion it was a good thing you didn't," said Medford. "If you had, you might have caught it dead center. As it was, two inches to the right and you'd have been a goner."

"Possibly," Slade admitted. "But I still feel I was outsmarted. The hellion is chain lightning on the draw and his mind works with hairtrigger speed and the precision of a machine. He was on the pull the instant he turned around; didn't have to see what was going on to know.

"Somehow," he added reflectively, "the devil reminds me of somebody, his methods, his general appearance, although of course I only got a glimpse of him, but just the same he seemed familiar. I keep wondering how he would look without that false nose and without the stain on his skin, but it won't come to me. Not so far, at least."

"It'll come, sooner or later, it always does for you," said Medford. "Always does. Well,

I'm going out and look things over; business is beginning to pick up, and this is nothing to what tonight will be."

"And I think I'll prowl around a bit," Slade replied. "Might be able to learn something."

"Watch your step," Medford cautioned. "No telling what the hellion has cooked up for you. About now he ain't feeling exactly in love with you."

7

As he sauntered through the busy streets, Slade was impressed by the way the town was growing. A few years before, a traveler had described Laredo as a very plain city whose prevailing style of architecture utilized stone or sun-dried brick walls and thatched roofs.

All that was changing. Now in the business section were going up white face brick and stone buildings dazzlingly reflecting the sunshine and giving emphasis to an atmosphere of cleanliness. Streets of the business section gave way to wide avenues where fine residences were being built. However, there were still drab *jacales,* adobe huts and squat houses of limestone. For the most part the structures were in good repair despite their age, and windows and door casings were painted in splashes of brilliant color.

He gazed at the graceful sweep of the International Bridge at the foot of Convent

Avenue. Even that had been improved on. A plan Slade suggested had been adopted and in place of solid steel sheets, removable aluminum railings had been constructed, which, when the Rio Grande was on the rampage, could be removed and carried to safety within thirty minutes. Stripped in this manner, the bridge presented virtually no obstruction to the current and its accumulation of floating debris that formerly impounded the rising waters, flooded Nuevo Laredo and reached such a height that only the tops of the high lamp-posts were visible. The time would come, Slade was firmly convinced, when more than fifty percent of all freight crossing the International Border would be handled through the Laredo port.

Progress! Greed and lawlessness must not prevail. The inhabitants of the town and the valley must be allowed to live without fear. Slade was glad to have the chance of furthering this desirable condition. Already he had done much; he was determined to do more. Such vermin as Loco Lobo and his brand must be exterminated. They would be!

The sun set in flame and splendor, the twilight deepened, the night came down. And Laredo began to really hum. The hundreds of irrigation workers crowded the bars and thronged the streets. Cowboys from the nearer spreads, and some from spreads not so near, rode in to lend a hand. Townspeople rallied to do their part. Laredo was always on the lookout for something to celebrate and the payday bust provided plenty of opportunity of various sorts.

El Halcón was thoroughly enjoying himself. Young, vigorous, he welcomed such nights, especially after long days of lonely riding. Meanwhile he studied faces, listening to conversations, but learned nothing he considered of importance. Finally, feeling hungry, he made his way to the Montezuma in quest of something to eat.

The sheriff was not present when he entered, but Gorty, the owner, said he expected him shortly.

"Place is jam-packed," he observed, "but I always save that little table at the corner for you and Tobe; figured you'd be in shortly. Old Doc was here a little while ago, wanted to know why you weren't bringing him some business. I told him the night was young, just wait."

Chuckling, he led the way to the table in question and beckoned a waiter to take Slade's order. "Roof," he said, which Slade knew to be waiter-and-owner jargon for "on the house."

El Halcón liked the table, for it gave him a good view of both the bar and the swinging doors, and a window that opened onto an alley, without being in line with it.

The Montezuma was jam-packed, all right, and the irrigation boys were whooping it up for fair, a number of cowhands rendering able assistance.

Sheriff Medford arrived while Slade was eating. He occupied a chair, ordered a meal and a snort to hold it down with.

"Anything new?" he asked.

"Nothing I've been able to note," the Ranger replied. "But as Gorty said, the night's still early. What's on your mind?" For the sheriff looked reflective.

"I was just wondering," he replied, "if that blasted Loco Lobo knows you are a Ranger?"

"I rather doubt it," Slade answered. "In fact, I don't think he knows much of anything relative to my background, unless perhaps my reputation in certain quarters for horning in on good things other people have started. Otherwise, I don't believe he would have made that try for the irrigation payroll money."

The sheriff looked bewildered. "Now what the devil do you mean by that?"

"Remember that slip of paper you found

in the dead outlaw's pocket?" Slade said. "That was a very accurately drawn plat of the irrigation project, pinpointing the location of the office building in which the payroll money would be kept over night. You will recall me mentioning that I was of the opinion that the man in question had been an individual of much more than average intelligence, quite likely well educated. I think that he had perhaps once been employed in some capacity that had to do with surveying or some other branch of engineering. Possibly a transit-man or a rod-man, who was able to read the plat and follow the outlined directions. He was the man supposed to handle the chore of tying onto the payroll. All right. Lobo would reasonably assume that we would find the plat in the course of examining the body. If he did have a knowledge of my background, knew me to be an engineer, he would have known that I would be able to decipher the plat, understand its function, and react accordingly. So he would have abandoned the project. Instead, with his subordinate out of the running, he took over the chore himself. I fear we can't hope for a second slip of a similar nature; the chances are he's just a mite suspicious of me now, shrewd as he is. That is barring the faint possibility that he concluded I knew the payroll money was stashed in the office safe and was standing guard over it, perhaps having designs on it myself."

"Anyhow, you kept the sidewinder from tying onto it," the sheriff remarked consolingly.

"Yes, but I don't feel particularly proud of the part I played in the affair," Slade replied. "First, I miscalculated a little and as a result only the thick stocking cap he wore under his hat saved the guard from being killed. And if I'd been just a little later, the combination would have been drilled out, the safe cleaned and Lobo and his hellions off unscathed. Secondly, I let the devil beat me to the pull."

"Well, as you said, you had to give the blasted wind spiders a chance to surrender, the peace officer's handicap," Medford reminded him. Slade nodded but didn't appear much impressed.

Medford glanced around at the crowded room. "Say!" he exclaimed, "this looks like about the wildest yet; 'pears everybody is here. Betcha there'll be trouble before morning."

"Stranger things have happened," Slade agreed. "The boys are whooping it up, all right. Well, let them have their fun; they work hard and deserve it. And there's no telling what the morrow will bring forth. Just as well, perhaps, that we can't read the future; who wants to know if his throat is going to be cut."

"Or he's going to get married," the sheriff grunted, who apparently looked upon matrimony as an even greater evil, a viewpoint sometimes developed by confirmed bachelors on the wrong side of sixty. Slade chuckled and forebore expressing an opinion apropos of that somewhat delicate subject.

Looked like a wild night, undoubtedly, and apt to grow wilder as the redeye got in its licks. Slade studied the bar and the occupants of the tables, endeavoring to spot a face that conformed to his conception of what Loco Lobo would look like minus his disguise, arriving only at the conclusion that the hellion could be patronizing the Montezuma at the moment and nobody the wiser. It was a tantalizing quest, and one not conducive to mental equanimity.

Wouldn't be surprising if Lobo was around somewhere, for it was the kind of night that promised opportunity for his brand. Outside sounded a clatter of hoofs, wild whoops, and a stuttering of shots as exuberant cowhands peppered holes in the sky. A less innocent bit of gun play would attract little attention.

"I'm going down to Miguel's cantina for a while," he announced. "Doesn't seem to be anything promising here."

"Watch your step," the sheriff repeated his warning. "The devils may be looking for you."

"I hope so," Slade replied. "For I certainly don't know where to look for them."

Medford snorted profanity but refrained from arguing the point.

"Chances are I'll see you there a little later," he said as Slade rose to go.

As Slade expected it would be, the river-front was even more boisterous than up-town. Every saloon was jammed, and a hilarious, jostling throng filled the streets.

Miguel's cantina was no exception. The bar was packed three-deep, the dance floor so crowded the dancers could barely shuffle. But nobody seemed to mind.

Like John Gorty of the Montezuma, Miguel always reserved a small table by the dance floor for Slade and the sheriff. *El Halcón* sat down and ordered coffee. Marie was on the floor but when the number was over she joined Slade in a glass of wine.

"Only a minute to stay, darling," she said. "One of the busiest nights we ever had. The boys all want to dance and there aren't nearly enough girls to go around. Wish Rosa was here; she'd love it. Got to go, but I'll be seeing you every now and then."

She hurried back to the floor, leaving Slade to smoke and sip coffee and watch the dancers and the crowd. He lingered for a while but saw nothing he considered of interest. Pancho Garza, the knife man, strolled in and paused at the end of the bar. Slade waved a greeting, which Pancho returned with a flash of teeth as white and even as Slade's own, glanced around and departed. Slade abruptly arrived at a decision; didn't appear there was anything to be learned in the cantina. Waving to Marie, whose eyes followed him anxiously out the door, he left the cantina and headed for Convent Street and the approach to the International Bridge that led to Nuevo Laredo.

And as he walked slowly across the span, far enough behind that even the extraordinarily keen eyes of *El Halcón* did not note them, four purposeful figures stole along.

Slade liked Nuevo Laredo, which was always gay and colorful. *Peones* in sandals and steeple sombreros adorned with much silver, colored serapes flung across their shoulders, walked the narrow streets, and dark-eyed *senoritas* with a ready smile for the tall Ranger. Black-robed Brothers of the Orders swept past, their lips muttering. There were strolling troubadors in colorful costumes, who paused at the corners with a crowd quickly gathering around them, tossing small coins to the itinerant musicians.

The curio shops and sidewalk stands displayed Mexican curios, earthenware, baskets, serapes, and sombreros along with costly jewelry, rare perfumes, less expensive pottery, flowers, meats, fruits, and vegetables — the merchants hawking their wares in strident tones.

Slade entered a cantina where he was known. Over a glass of wine, he engaged Felipe, the owner, in conversation.

"Loco Lobo?" Felipe repeated in answer to Slade's question. "An evil man, a *muy malo hombre,* very bad, very bad. *Si,* he has been seen here in Nuevo Laredo. So far as I know, he has done nothing here to call to him the attention of the authorities, but he is not welcome. You seek him, *Capitan? Bueno!* His days are numbered. Him who *El Halcón* seeks, be he evil, is not long for this world."

Slade was inclined to be less optimistic. He felt that ushering Loco Lobo through the portals of the next world was likely to be a hefty chore. Saying goodnight to Felipe, he continued his stroll through the town, and ever the four furtive figures stole along in his wake.

Felipe's place was orderly, but there were others along the river that were less so, to put it mildly. Slade visited several, and saw nothing he considered of interest. He was about to abandon his quest as futile and return to Laredo when he approached a place that was somewhat dimly lighted but quieter than most. He hesitated a moment, then entered.

The room was not very large and not too crowded. There were a number of irrigation workers present, several cowhands from north of the river, and quite a few Mexican *vaqueros*. As he entered, a man standing midway along the bar turned toward him and he tensed for instant action.

It was Loco Lobo!

8

The recognition was instantly mutual. Loco Lobo's hand flickered to his holster. He was lightning fast, but not quite fast enough. A split second before he squeezed trigger, Slade's Colt spouted flame. Loco Lobo's bullet went wild. His gun thudded to the floor and he reeled back with a scream of pain and anger, whirled and dashed for a rear door. Slade tried to line sights again, but there were men between him and the target and he was forced to hold his fire. He bounded in pursuit and was engulfed in the frantic crowd seeking to avoid flying lead. Loco Lobo was through the door. An instant later a second door banged. Slade disgustedly drew back. Loco Lobo had escaped again!

The place was thoroughly in an uproar! Men were shouting, cursing, bellowing questions; some appeared to consider Slade the instigator of the ruckus. Eyes regarded him menacingly. The situation was just a trifle tense. Any moment somebody might take a chance despite the gun in his hand and he would have to shoot his way out of the rumhole.

Abruptly there were four men ranged alongside Slade. Foremost was Miguel's knife man, Pancho Garza. He held his long blade by the point and was gently swinging it to and fro. As the tumult hushed somewhat, he called pleasantly —

"*Hombres,* what would you? Know you not *El Halcón,* the good, the just, the friend of the lowly? He is my *amigo.* And," he added, his voice soft and deadly, "my blade does not miss!"

There was a moment of silence, then a burly irrigation worker whooped, "Neither does his bullet! He shot the gun outa that hellion's hand quicker'n a cat can lick its nose with its tongue already out!"

That broke the tension. A roar of laughter followed. Men who had been glaring at Slade grinned. The irrigation worker let out another bellow.

"Why, it's Mr. Slade! Us fellers are for him, too, and don't anybody forget it."

The owner, portly, moon-faced, came forward.

"I know not what it is all about," he said,

"but why not all drink, on the house, and forget?"

That was an offer any such gathering is slow to refuse. Everybody bellied up to the bar; the bartender got busy pouring. An irrigation worker approached Slade.

"Here's the feller's gun," he said. "Picked it up off the floor. One butt plate's smashed. Got a notion you knocked a hunk of meat outa his hand, too, from the way he yelped."

Slade thanked the worker and passed the gun to Pancho. "A good iron," he said. "Plate can be replaced. Keep it as a souvenir. And *gracias* for showing up at just the right time."

"In time to save some brainless ones from dying," Pancho replied, accepting the gift. "We know *El Halcón* likes not to kill when it is not necessary, so I reasoned gently with those *ladrones,* and they heeded."

Slade suppressed a grin; Pancho's "reasoning" was similar to that of a capped stick of dynamite with the fuse burning short.

"How come you showed up when you did?" he asked.

"All the night we have followed you, *Capitan,*" Pancho explained. "We were close behind you when you entered here, for this portion of the town is bad. We heard the shots and entered quickly. Just what did happen, *Capitan?*"

Slade told him. "Hitting his gun hand was just a fluke," he concluded. "I certainly didn't aim at it — he's too fast to take chances with."

"I see," said Pancho, "and he escaped."

"Yes, for the second time," Slade answered. "Hellion seems to bear a charmed life."

"Charmed it will not remain," Pancho declared confidently.

Slade's eyes grew thoughtful. "I wonder why he was here?" he remarked. "Why did he come to this particular place?" Pancho lowered his voice.

"I would say, *Capitan,* that he came here to meet with someone. I know this place. It is frequented by *ladrones* from both sides of the river."

"You may have something there," Slade agreed. "Perhaps he hoped to enlist some recruits. He has suffered rather heavy losses of late."

"Doubtless it is so," said Pancho. "Here I see faces I do not like. Not that we have aught to fear. The irrigation men are your friends, and so of course are the *vaqueros* now that they know you to be *El Halcón.* Did one seek to follow us when we leave, he would be but stepping into a grave."

Slade was inclined to agree; the *vaqueros,* Mexican cowboys, were a hard lot.

"Well, I think I've had enough of Nuevo Laredo for tonight," he said. "Suppose we amble across the bridge to Miguel's place?"

"Assuredly, *Capitan,*" replied Pancho. They waved goodbye to everybody and departed, voices calling well wishes after them.

"Do you think Loco Lobo seriously injured?" Pancho asked as they headed for the bridge.

"Some skin knocked off his hand is about all, the chances are," Slade answered. "Sure didn't slow him down when he hightailed; you could hear him whiz."

"Doubtless next time he will show less speed," Pancho predicted cheerfully. Slade hoped he was right.

When they reached Miguel's cantina, without mishap, they found it still going strong. Marie regarded them accusingly as they filed in, but was too busy to ask questions, at the moment. Miguel had a jovial welcome and a freshly opened bottle of wine. He seemed to sense that something had happened, drew Pancho aside and engaged him in conversation. Slade occupied his little table and ordered coffee to go with the wine.

All considered, the night hadn't been too bad, even though he did miss another opportunity to rid the section of Loco Lobo. At least he had given the pest a slight lesson in gun handling, proving to him that, fast as he was, there could be men in the world just a mite faster. At the moment the outlaw leader was very likely nursing a sore hand and wounded pride. The irritation developing might cause him to recklessly do something foolish. Not that Slade was overly sanguine as to that; Loco Lobo's shrewd, calculating brain would probably deter him from going off half-cocked.

Given to reflecting on the importance of seemingly trivial incidents, he recalled that the night before he himself had been within two inches of eternity. Tonight the difference of an inch in the position of Loco Lobo's gun hand was the difference between life and death for the outlaw.

Marie joined him. "All right, let's have it," she said. "I know something terrible happened. Pancho came in looking as smug as a cat that's just finished a saucer of cream."

He told her. "That awful man!" she exclaimed, and repeated his former remark, "It seems he bears a charmed life."

Slade was tempted to repeat Pancho's observation relative to the charmed life of

Loco Lobo, but refrained.

"How's it going here?" he asked.

"Fine, but frightfully busy," she answered. "I don't mind, though, it's interesting and exciting. The irrigation boys are nice, and some of them have a delicious sense of humor. Romantically inclined, of course, and in most cases, as Mr. Dickens phrased it, 'Barkis is willin'.' Shut up!"

"I didn't say a word," he protested.

"No, but you looked it. Present company is excepted."

"Lack of willingness is sometimes based on lack of opportunity," he observed judiciously.

Miss Telo tossed her curls, and fell into the trap. "Oh, I don't lack for opportunity," she replied airily.

"Nor for willingness," he retorted pointedly.

"*Touché!*" she giggled. "Pour me a drink."

Sheriff Medford stalked in and the story of the night's incident was repeated for his benefit.

"And the hellion got in the clear again, eh?" he growled.

"Yes, he did," Slade replied. "I thought for a moment I had him, but it didn't work out that way; he's good at getting the breaks."

"He'll have his blasted neck busted by a hangman's knot, if he don't lean against the hot end of a slug," declared Medford. "And you think he was there to round up a few wind spiders for his bunch?"

"Taking into consideration what Pancho said, I'm inclined to think so," Slade conceded.

"Which means you've sorta got him on the run."

"Possibly," Slade agreed. "At least his style has been cramped a little; he may not have many of his original bunch left. But he's a host unto himself.

"And, blast it!" he added, "again I got only a glimpse of him in that dim light; but the feeling persists that I've seen him someplace before, although I still can't for the life of me call to mind where or under what circumstances. Perhaps, however, it is only a resemblance, although I still don't admit that is the answer."

"Will come to you, perhaps in a way you'll least expect," said Medford.

Marie went back to the floor for a couple of numbers. Slade and the sheriff sat on at the table, smoking and talking. The crowd was thinning out, for the hour was growing late and Nature was taking toll. Already Miguel was glancing suggestively at the clock, the girls expectantly at their partners. Nearly all the gaming tables were now vacant, the roulette wheels had ceased to whirl, the faro bank had shut up shop. The bartenders wearily poured drinks for the die-hards. The payday bust was drawing to a close.

"And so far, I haven't heard of any bad trouble," said the sheriff. "Guess the only real trouble was in Nuevo Laredo; sorta follows *El Halcón* around. And here comes your trouble, looking for you. Poor gal 'pears tired, and no wonder."

"I'm not too tired," Marie, who had overheard the remark, said cheerfully. She also glanced at the clock.

9

A little after noon the following day, Slade got the rig on Shadow and rode west by north on the river trail. He planned to put a theory to the test — a theory based on Loco Lobo's custom of murdering and robbing lonely horsemen riding the trail through the sparsely inhabited section where he had first made contact with some of Lobo's bunch.

He theorized that somewhere in the brush country to the north of the trail at that point the outlaws had a hole-up where they could lie low after forays. To the north, east, and west of Laredo were prosperous cattle ranches. To the east was the most favorable terrain for cows, but the pasture to the north and west was also good. It was from those spreads that horsemen rode the river trail on their way to Laredo.

There were game tracks through the belt of brushland, and occasional trails beaten out in years gone by Indians who raided into Mexico. Scattered through the brush were old cabins once occupied by hunters and trappers.

Slade reasoned that one of these isolated and never-visited shacks might well be the hangout of the outlaws. Could he locate it, there would be a chance to bag the whole bunch at one swoop. First, however, he must locate it, which promised to be something of a chore. To hit on the right spot in that jumble of thorny growth was like trying to pick a particular tick from a sheep's back. But he had been successful on such quests before and it was not beyond the realm of the possible that he would be again.

He rode alert and watchful, constantly scanning the terrain in all directions, carefully noting the movements of birds on the wing and little animals scurrying in and out of the brush. More than once, in the past, these furred or feathered friends had warned him of peril and saved him from disaster. Also, he paid particular heed to the reactions of his horse. Keen as was his hearing, Shadow could hear sounds that failed to register in his master's ears. A sudden snort or a soft blowing through his nose would set *El Halcón* very much on the *qui vive*.

As he approached the long rise beyond the crest of which he'd had the ruckus with the drygulchers, his vigilance increased. However, there was no sign of life other than the little critters who belonged. Topping the sag, he slowed Shadow and intently studied the growth to his right. Abruptly he drew rein. Broken twigs were dangling from the chaparral.

"This is where those two hellions holed up," he remarked to Shadow. "But they didn't come through the brush here. If there's a way through that horses can negotiate without difficulty, I'd say it's some distance farther west, by which the five that followed me reached the trail. Okay, horse, we'll go see." He rode on slowly, constantly scanning the trail ahead, but also giving careful study to the encroaching growth.

Covering a couple of miles and discovering nothing, he topped another rise and saw that in the far distance the belt of chaparral narrowed and thinned, to be replaced by the rolling rangeland.

"Should be close, if there is such a thing," he remarked. "Keep your eyes skinned, horse, and your ears open." Shadow snorted, as much as to say, "Don't I always? You pay a little better attention to what's going on and we'll be okay." Slade chuckled and rode on. Another half mile and abruptly he reined to a stop. Directly opposite where he sat, near the crest of another rise, was a narrow opening in the growth, little more than a game track. Dismounting, he went down on hands and knees and studied the ground. The surface was hard and flinty, but the eyes of *El Halcón* missed nothing. He straightened up.

"This is it," he said. "Horses have come out of this crack recently, and I'm darned if it doesn't look like cows have also." He turned and gazed south to the nearby river. Here the stream was smooth and placid save for a plainly discernible ripple that extended from bank to bank.

"Indications are of a ford," he announced. "Perhaps a ledge something like the Indian Crossing north of Bruni Street in Laredo. That's a ledge of limestone rock lying just below the surface of the water, and in dry seasons part of it becomes exposed. Was known to the Indian tribes long before white men discovered it. They used it to cross cattle and horses stolen from settlers and sold in Mexico. This could be somewhat similar, and perhaps used for a similar purpose. I wonder?"

Shadow, who had unpleasant memories anent the Indian Crossing, gave a disgusted snort — "Here we go again, eh?"

"Not this time, I'd say," Slade reassured

him. "Right now we're going to try and learn where that old Indian trail through the brush leads. To something interesting, I've a notion. All right, in you go."

Entering the growth, Slade rode with the greatest caution, pausing often to peer and listen before rounding one of the many turns. Now the stony soil at the mouth of the trail was replaced by a spongy surface that instantly sprang back after being trodden, from which Shadow's irons gave back but a whisper of sound. So he was almost caught unawares when, easing around a bend, he came face to face with a horseman riding in the opposite direction.

The fellow gave a yelp of alarm, jerked his horse to a halt and went for his gun.

Slade drew and shot. He shot to wound, not to kill for he wished to take the man alive. But just as he pulled trigger the frightened horse reared and the fellow caught the slug about eight inches lower than *El Halcón* had intended. He fell from the saddle without a sound.

Instantly, heedless of thorns and trailing branches, Slade backed Shadow into the dense wall of chaparral and sat listening. Were there anybody near, the shot must have most assuredly been heard.

But as the minutes dragged past, no

menacing sound broke the hushed peace of nature. Alarmed birds settled back into the thickets. A rodent stole across the track, showing no indication of fear. Slade waited a few more minutes, then pushed back to the trail and dismounted.

The dead man had an unfamiliar face, a hard-lined countenance and glazed eyes that gave an impression of muddiness. An unsavory specimen, all right, the Ranger was relieved to recognize. Would not be pleasant to have downed a harmless cowboy taking a short cut by way of the trail. But the fellow's hands showed no indications of his having worked at anything recently, and his pockets divulged rather more money than a puncher would be likely to pack.

"And anyhow, we didn't have much choice," he told Shadow. "He was on the prod, all right, and I was forced to beat him to it."

After another spell of listening, he dragged the body into the chaparral and covered it with brush. Removing the horse's rig, he served it likewise. What to do with the critter, he had no idea. The horse proceeded to simplify matters somewhat by following him when he resumed his cautious ride.

He had covered but a short distance when to his sensitive nostrils came a faint whiff of smoke, as from a fire that had almost burned out. Halting instantly, he again listened for any sound from ahead. None came; the hush of the wastelands still held sway.

"Just the same, I'm not going to risk more of your clumping," he told Shadow. Turning the cayuse's nose, he forced it into the growth for a little distance, glancing back uneasily at the outlaw's horse that might well give everything away. However the critter, doubtless trained to do so, followed obediently and paused alongside Shadow when Slade dismounted and dropped the split reins to the ground. Both animals stood motionless; looked like that immediate problem was solved, for the time being, at least.

On foot, *El Halcón* stole ahead. The trail made one of its sudden turns and a moment later he found himself at the edge of a rather small clearing where only an occasional straggle of low brush grew. And in the middle of the clearing was an ancient cabin that still looked quite tight as to walls and roof. A closed door and a smeary window faced him. To all appearances the shack was deserted, but a faint trickle of smoke rising from the stick-and-mud chimney hinted at recent occupancy, quite likely by the man he met on the trail.

For long minutes he stood watching and listening. Nothing happened and he heard no sound. He decided to take a chance. With quick light steps he covered the few yards to the cabin, a rather nerve-wracking business, and sighed with relief when he reached the wall near the window. Edging along, he peered in. There was nobody in the single room. He pushed the door open and entered.

The cabin was a hangout, all right, similar to others he had discovered in his time. There were several bunks built along the wall, all but one fairly new, staple provisions on shelves, and tin plates and mugs. There was a bucket of fresh water beside the stone fireplace. Very likely the shack had been used by more than one bunch during recent years.

What interested Slade more, neatly stacked on a table were six tin plates and six tin cups, and a bundle of knives and forks. Looked a little like the gent now sleeping peacefully under his cover of brush had expected company.

A pot of coffee simmered invitingly on the last of the coals in the fireplace. Slade chanced pouring and downing a cup. He rinsed the cup, replaced it on a shelf and left the cabin without delay, not relishing the likelihood of the bunch catching him there.

Outside, he scanned the clearing. Behind the cabin was a lean-to that would accommodate half a dozen horses. At the moment it was empty. Nearby a spring bubbled. And to the north of the clearing the trail continued through the wall of brush. Slade determined to try and learn where it led; might have a bearing on the future moves of the outlaws. He hurried back to Shadow, led him from the brush and mounted. The outlaw's horse continued to follow.

Entering the brush once more, he continued to ride north. A little more than a mile and the trail narrowed until it would hardly accommodate two horses abreast. A few more minutes and it narrowed still a bit more, reached a final straggle of overhanging brush and opened onto rangeland. In the distance, Slade could see clumps of grazing cattle. He glanced back the way he had come. The opening in the growth was so narrow, so obscured by interlaced and overhanging branches that one riding within a few yards of it would not be aware of its existence.

Not far off ran a little stream. The outlaw's horse trotted to it, sucked up a swig and began grazing up the stream, paying no more attention to him, which suited *El Halcón* precisely.

Gazing across the rangeland, Walt Slade did some hard and fast thinking. He experienced a presentiment that something was going to happen, that the outlaws had something in mind and would quite probably gather in the hangout sometime during the night. He didn't feel quite up to tackling the whole bunch, the odds being somewhat lopsided. But he sensed opportunity. He estimated he was not much more than fifteen miles from Laredo, all told, and Shadow was fresh. Turning the cayuse, he rode back the way he had come, at a fast pace, slowed up as he reached the clearing. A glance around showed nothing inimical. He paused long enough to allow Shadow to drink from the spring, then speeded up once more.

Riding the winding track through the brush was not exactly pleasant and he was relieved when he reached the river trail without incident. It stretched deserted, east and west. He glanced at the sun, which was nearing the horizon, and continued on his way, reaching town shortly past full dark. After caring for Shadow, he hurried to the sheriff's office, found Medford in and informed him of what he had discovered.

"It may be just the chance we've been hoping for," he concluded. "If we can manage to catch the bunch in that cabin, there's every reason to believe we should make a clean sweep."

"You're darn right!" Medford agreed heartily. "When do we start?"

"No hurry." Slade replied. "I want Shadow to have a couple of hours rest at least. We have plenty of time to eat and take it easy for a spell. In fact, I don't consider it advisable to ride out of town too early."

"Expect you're right," said Medford. "Figure you can find that crack in the brush in the dark?"

"I have no doubt," Slade answered. "I spotted several landmarks, and that ripple in the river, denoting, I think, a ford, will show plainly in the starlight, and there'll be a late moon, too." The sheriff nodded and tugged his mustache.

"Don't suppose they might be suspicious when that wind spider you downed turns up missing?"

"Not likely, I'd say," Slade said. "They could hardly be expected to divine what happened to him. More likely to think he just rode off somewhere, as he was doing when I met him, and got held up. That sort is seldom dependable. I don't believe he would have been riding to meet the others; would have been no reason to do so, or at least that's how I size up the situation. But we'll take care they don't get the jump on us."

"Little chance of that with you on the job," said Medford. "Shall we go eat as soon as I round up my deputies? I know where to find 'em."

"Tell them to meet us here three hours from now," Slade decided.

Medford hurried out. Slade settled himself comfortably to await his return.

He was back very shortly. "All set," he announced. "Let's go eat. The Montezuma?"

"Good as any," Slade replied. "We'll hang around there for a while, so if anybody happens to be keeping tabs on us, which I consider unlikely, they'll conclude we're all set for the night."

10

With the stars wanly silvering the river trail, Slade, the sheriff, and the three deputies rode out of Laredo. Some distance from town, they paused while Slade scanned the back trail. Satisfied they were not followed, he gave the order to proceed and they rode on through the quiet of the night. The track lay deserted, the occasional calls of night birds and the distant yipping of coyotes seeming to accentuate its loneliness. Slade had no difficulty locating the opening in the growth where the old Indian track began. They turned into it and headed north.

Nobody particularly enjoyed that slow ride through the black dark, with no way of telling what they might meet with around one of the many turns. Even Slade felt relieved when with his uncanny instinct for distance and direction, he called a halt at almost the spot where he had concealed Shadow some hours before.

"From now on we take it on foot," he said in low tones. "Can't take a chance with the cayuses. Into the brush with them."

The horses, except Shadow, were tethered to convenient trunks and told to keep quiet. The posse stole forward until they reached the clearing.

The old cabin stood dark and silent, with no sign of movement anywhere. Slade could see the lean-to was untenanted, pretty good evidence the outlaws were not present.

"Maybe they're asleep," breathed the sheriff.

"Not likely," Slade replied. "I'd say they just haven't arrived yet. Spread out in the shadow of the brush and wait, that's all we can do. I have a feeling they'll show before long."

But as the tedious minutes dragged past with nothing happening, he began to wonder a bit uneasily if his hunch, after all, wasn't a straight one. Or if the outlaws had grown suspicious because of the absence of the man left in the cabin and had already arrived and departed. Nearly half an hour passed and the conviction that he had guessed wrong strengthened.

And then suddenly his keen ears caught a sound he at once identified as the bleat of a steer, some distance away. And *El Halcón* understood.

"Listen!" he exclaimed. "The devils have widelooped a herd of cows and aim to run them across the Rio Grande to Mexico by way of that ford I mentioned. Chances are they'll stop here awhile to let the cattle rest a bit before shoving them on south. Wait till they're bunched behind the herd. You do the talking, Tobe. We have to give them a chance to surrender. I don't think they'll take it, so if the ball opens, shoot fast and shoot straight. Get set, they'll show in another five minutes."

Tense and eager, the posse waited, guns ready for action. Suddenly a dark shape loomed on the far side of the clearing, another and another. Soon there were around a hundred head of stock milling in the clearing. A rider appeared, and another, until they numbered five all told. As Slade expected, they bunched together, slowing their horses. He nudged the sheriff. Medford's voice rang out —

"Up! You're covered! In the name of the law —"

His voice was drowned by a chorus of alarmed exclamations. Slade saw hands flash to holsters. He drew and shot with both Colts.

A blazing gun battle ensued. Yells, curses,

the booming of the guns, the hissing of lead, and the bawling of the terrified cattle raised a hideous pandemonium to the shuddering stars.

Slade saw a man fall. A grunt sounded behind him and he knew one of the deputies was hit. A slug just touched the top of his own shoulder. Another ripped through the crown of his hat.

The outlaws fought back viciously, but the advantage was with the men on foot and in the shadow. A second saddle was emptied. A voice rang out above the turmoil. The remaining three whirled their mounts and tore back into the brush, the riderless horses galloping after them. Slade raced across the clearing, dodging the bewildered, milling cows, paused at the mouth of the trail, listening. He heard the beat of hoofs fading into the north with no let-up.

Sheriff Medford panted alongside him. "Not bad, not bad," he chortled. "We've got the cows they stole and knocked off two of the horned toads. Not bad at all."

"But I'm willing to wager Loco Lobo isn't one of the two," Slade returned disgustedly. "That was him let out the yell before they went into the brush. Hellion made it in the clear again!"

"His time's on the way," the sheriff predicted cheerfully. "Got a notion he's at about the end of his twine. Shall we look over what we've bagged?"

"First," Slade said, "is anybody badly hurt? I thought somebody got nicked."

"Oh, Alf's got a streak burned along his neck, nothing to worry about," Medford replied. "Knocked him sorta silly for a minute, but he's all right now."

"There are a couple of bracket lamps in that cabin, go get them," Slade ordered the deputies. They hurried to obey and shortly returned with the lamps lighted.

The dead owlhoots proved to be of an average type, so far as Slade could judge, typical of the Border breed. There was nothing in their pockets save considerable money, which the sheriff confiscated.

Next they gave the cows, that were now contentedly grazing, a once-over.

"Why, they're some of Si Brenner's S Bar B stock," said Medford, after a glance at the brands. "You say that track leads north to the rangeland? Then I'd say his casa ain't more'n four or five miles to the northwest. Shall we run the critters back there and spend the night with Si? He's as cantankerous as a centipede with chillblains, but not a bad sort; an old bach."

"A good idea," Slade agreed. "First,

though, while the critters are resting and filling their bellies, we might as well take over that shack and rustle a surrounding. Plenty of good chuck in there. Cup of hot coffee wouldn't go bad about now."

"Fine!" exclaimed Medford. "I'm feelin' sorta lank. Don't figure those sidewinders might come back?"

"I think we can risk it," Slade answered. He examined the deputy's bullet-scorched neck and decided the wound was of little consequence. However, he whistled to Shadow, who came trotting into the clearing, snorting his disapproval of things in general, and applied a bandage and a couple of strips of plaster.

A sack of oats was found under the lean-to and the horses provided for. One of the deputies was a good cook and soon had a hefty surrounding on the table, the stacked plates and mugs coming in handy. Then, after a smoke, they lined up the thoroughly irritated cows and headed them north on the brush trail. Reaching the rangeland, they turned north by west and after a couple of hours drive sighted the S Bar B casa. Their bleating charges were shoved close and Medford hammered on the door.

"Who the heck is it?" sounded a muffled voice inside.

"Open up, Brenner," shouted the sheriff. "This is the Law."

"Who the blankety-blank gives a blankety-blank for the blankety-blank Law at this time of the night!" came an indignant howl from within.

"Open up!" bawled the sheriff.

There was a thumping of bare feet on the floor, the door was opened to reveal a white-whiskered, night-gowned old gent with an irascible countenance and brandishing a cocked sawed-off shotgun. There was a hurried scattering to get out of line with the twin muzzles.

"What the blinkin' blue blazes?" demanded Brenner in a voice that shook the rafters.

"We just drove in a hundred and better of your stock," the sheriff told him. "What do you mean by lettin' 'em stray all the way to Laredo and clutter up the streets?"

"Tobe Medford," the other screeched, "I always knew you'd crack up sooner or later. Finally happened, eh? Who are those loco gents with you? Come in, come in, even crazy as you are you must be cold out there. I'll have your critters taken care of." He let loose another of his stentorian bellows, which really wasn't necessary, for, aroused by the tumult, most of the hands were already outside the bunkhouse. Several came hurrying forward, one was introduced to Shadow and the big black and the others were led to the barn.

"Roscoe!" boomed Brenner as they filed in. A couple of minutes and a second old gent, even whiter whiskered and more cantankerous-looking than the first appeared.

"What the blankety-blank do you mean by waking a man up in the middle of the night?" he squealed in a high falsetto.

"Coffee!" ordered Brenner. "Can't you see these horned toads are freezin'?"

"All right," piped Roscoe, "and tomorrow I'm askin' for my time!"

"You won't get it," Brenner told him. "Rustle your hocks!"

Roscoe, squeaking profanity, stumped off to the kitchen.

"Been with me for better'n forty years," said Brenner. "Couldn't think more of him if he was my own brother. Now, Tobe, tell me what really happened."

Medford told him, starting at the beginning and giving Slade the credit due.

"So that's where my cows have been going!" Brenner exclaimed, when the sheriff paused. "A fine chore, Mr. Slade, a fine chore! Much obliged; the loss of that herd would have set me back considerable." He stretched out a gnarled paw.

Shortly, the coffee, steaming hot, was served by the irascible Roscoe who nevertheless, Slade noted, had a twinkle in his eye. He grinned at the Ranger and was rewarded with the flashing white smile of *El Halcón* which men, and women, found irresistible.

After coffee was downed, Brenner said, "Tobe, you and Slade can sleep here in the casa. There's room for your boys in the bunkhouse. Now suppose we go to bed; I crave shut-eye. Sure I'll let you have horses to pack the bodies in: the boys can pick them up later."

The following morning, after a hearty breakfast and more thanks from Si Brenner, the posse headed for Laredo. When they reached the point where the trail emptied into the clearing, Slade called a halt and for some minutes sat scanning the terrain. Birds were flitting about, showing no signs of alarm; all appeared silent and deserted.

"But best not to take chances," he observed. "I wouldn't put anything past Lobo."

"You're darn right," growled the sheriff. "He's a snake-blooded devil of the first water or there never was one."

The two bodies were roped to the spare

horses and the journey to town resumed.

They made something of a triumphant entry into Laredo and soon the sheriff's office was packed with people wishing to view the dead outlaws. Among them was Pancho Garza, Miguel's knife man. He drew Slade aside.

"All three I have seen, *Capitan,* in Nuevo Laredo," he announced. "They we could do without. However, they always seemed to behave themselves and the *alcalde* and the *jefe politico* did not bother them."

Which Slade could understand. The authorities of the Mexican town were complacent and welcomed trade from north of the river. Not surprising that the hellions were not questioned or expelled.

What interested him most was the fact that it appeared Nuevo Laredo was in the nature of a hangout for the bunch — which he put in the back of his mind for future reference. Of course, he had no authority in the Mexican town, but, as the old saying went, "Judge Colt holds court on the Rio Grande!" — which applied to both shores of that river.

"Thinning 'em out, thinning 'em out," the sheriff remarked complacently.

"Yes, but Loco Lobo is still on the loose, and until he is corraled the chore is really just begun," Slade reminded him.

"Uh-huh, that's right, but he's suffered more setbacks in the past few days than he did before during all the months he's been operating in the section," said Medford. "I still say you've got him on the run."

"Maybe, but he sure seems to run fast," Slade returned dryly. "Seems almost able to outrun a slug, at least where I'm concerned. Three times I thought I had him lined up, and three times he got in the clear."

"Won't last," Medford predicted confidently. "Well, now what? What say we amble over to the Montezuma for a snack? I've about digested my breakfast."

"I'm in favor of it," Slade replied. "Let's go!"

Although sunset was still some time off, the Montezuma was already doing plenty of business.

Seemed everybody wished to hear about the frustrated widelooping and the downing of the two outlaws. Soon their table was surrounded by a curious crowd, shooting questions.

The sheriff obliged, and he was a good story teller. His hearers lived with him through that thundering gun battle in the clearing and thrilled to the mad flight of the three who escaped, expressing regret that they did escape, and showering Slade with compliments. Finally, however, they drifted away and the two peace officers were left to enjoy their dinner in peace.

"Lobo is sure full of surprises," Slade remarked reminiscently as they ate. "He's a master of the unexpected. The last thing I counted on was a chore of rustling, although on that track through the brush I did note signs of cattle having passed that way. I figured the bunch were planning a get-together in the cabin. Came very nearly getting caught flat-footed. Seems the hellion is always a jump ahead of me."

"He was sure a jump ahead of all of us when he skalley-hooted," Medford observed dryly. "I can still hear him whiz."

"But the fact that he was able to stay ahead of us puts him still a *jump* ahead," Slade replied. "We've still got to close the gap."

"We'll close it," Medford said cheerfully.

"Master of the unexpected," Slade suddenly repeated reflectively. "Somehow that, too, strikes a chord of memory." He sat silent for some moments, his eyes seeming to gaze into the far distances.

"What you thinking about, Walt?" the sheriff asked curiously.

"A line from Swinburne," Slade answered.

" 'That dead men rise up never.' I wonder!"

The sheriff looked puzzled, but *El Halcón* did not see fit, at the moment, to elaborate his cryptic remark.

And Medford knew that at the moment he *was El Halcón,* inscrutable as the great mountain hawk for which he was named, predatory, almost — with eyes that looked beyond the mental horizon, probing, analyzing, dissecting, viewing the dismembered parts dispassionately, the vague angles of the problem which confronted him. Ultimately he always arrived at the right conclusion. Tobe Medford had learned to respect those silences, although they were mostly beyond his comprehension. Walt Slade would talk when he was ready, not before. When he did speak, his remark did not tend to enlighten the sheriff —

"Swinburne could have been wrong."

Medford shook his head and refrained from asking questions.

After a while they pushed back their empty plates and lighted pipe and cigarette, smoking in silence as the manner of men full-fed and relaxed.

"Guess I'd better mosey down to Miguel's cantina," Slade observed.

"A good idea," agreed the sheriff. "Imagine your gal had a case of the jitters last night, but Pancho must have told her you are all right and she'll be all set to give you a scolding; women are so darned contrary."

11

The sunset was painting the sky with its never palling wonder of color when Slade left the Montezuma. He walked slowly, marveling at the changing beauty. A few clouds were edged with gold that blended slowly to royal purple overspread with a film of rose. The upper curve of the great orb sank below the horizon as he reached the cantina, paused a moment, then entered.

The sheriff proved to be no mean prophet. Marie did scold him for exposing himself to danger.

"But I haven't much choice," he protested. "It's my work."

"Yes, I suppose so," she sighed, "and you always seem to come through all right, but I can't help worrying."

"Nice that I am so much in your thoughts," he rallied. Marie sniffed daintily.

"Sometimes I wonder if you appreciate it," she said. "Oh, well, I suppose it could be worse. At least your eyes don't rove over the dance floor as much as they used to."

"They never did," he declared. Marie sniffed again.

"Nothing wrong with my eyesight," she observed pointedly. "Not that I blame you over much; some of them are cute."

Which ended that phase of the conversation.

Miguel came over with a bottle of wine and congratulations. "People breathe easier, *Capitan,* thanks to you," he said. "They say the menace of Loco Lobo will soon be of the past."

"Here's hoping," replied Slade, raising his glass. "But he's still in the clear, and he's a slippery customer."

"The slip he will make that will slip him out of this world," Miguel said placidly. "Drink hearty, *Capitan,* drink hearty, *caro mio,* the night is young and the stars shine brightly. Let love guide the way, and fear not for the future." He ambled off, leaving Slade chuckling, and Marie smiling a trifle wistfully.

Marie went on the floor for a couple of numbers. Slade sat smoking and thinking. He experienced a rising exultation, for he believed that at long last he had the answer to the perplexing and highly irritating question of whom Loco Lobo reminded him, both in appearance and method of operating. It seemed incredible, but he was becoming more and more convinced that it was so.

That a man could go into the "Black Water," that sullen, snake- and alligator-infested stream in the Big Thicket of East Texas, at night, and live, defied comprehension; but it appeared the hellion did.

Yes, he was certain he had the answer, and he understood to the full the problem he was up against.

Well, twice he had the devil on the run, even though he did manage to slide out of the loop both times. Perhaps history would repeat, with possibly a more satisfactory ending.

He mulled over something at which he had never ceased to marvel, the importance of trifles. A chance phrase of his own uttering, "master of the unexpected," had flung wide the gates of memory. More than once he had employed that phrase, vocally or mentally, in describing the man in question. He *was* master of the unexpected. The attempted rustling of Si Brenner's cattle the night before was an example — the last thing he, Slade, had expected him to do.

Well, anyhow, he now knew who Loco

Lobo was, and he was ready to confide in the sheriff.

A little later the old peace officer put in an appearance. He slumped into a chair and ordered a snort.

"Say!" he exclaimed querulously, "I can't get over what you quoted from that fool poet, Swineherd, or whatever his name was. Just what did you mean by that about dead men not rising up?"

Slade laughed. "I fear Mr. Swinburne would not be flattered by your rendition of his name," he replied. "All right, I'll explain.

"Up in the Panhandle, nearly two years back, I met a man who called himself Tobar Shaw. The most ruthless, cleverest, and most far-seeing outlaw leader I ever encountered. He was unique, a shadow, a phantom — and as I said, a master of the unexpected. Also, a master of organization. He was utterly snake-blooded, killed for the pleasure of killing. A man of culture and education who undoubtedly knew quite a bit about geology and kindred subjects. He had his eye on a piece of property his geological knowledge convinced him was of great potential value, with which I agree. He schemed to obtain it, meanwhile going in for robbery, burglary, widelooping, and murder. As I said, he was unique, and amazingly clever. He had me fooled to the very last. Suffice it to say, I, with the help of the sheriff of Potter County, managed to clean out his bunch, and I thought I had him in my loop. I chased him across the Tucumcari Desert and was overtaking him when one of the infernal dust storms peculiar to the region all of a sudden blew up. Under cover of it he escaped. I was confident he'd come back to Texas again and begin operating somewhere."

"Did he?" asked the sheriff, much interested.

"Yes, he did," Slade continued. "He showed up at Beaumont and the Spindletop oil field. Along with his other talents, he was a master of disguises. He grew a heavy beard, dyed it black, along with his hair, which was naturally on the yellow side, peered through thick-lensed glasses — the lenses very likely nothing but window glass — hunched his square shoulders and unusually straight back, and adopted the name of Turner Shane. He had gotten together another bunch of hellions more intelligent than most, and raised the very devil in Jefferson County and adjoining counties."

"Sounds like a real sidewinder," interpolated the sheriff.

"He was, and is," Slade replied. "While

there, he pulled off the most brazen and outstanding stealing I ever heard of; he stole an oil well, no less. I'll give you the details of that later. Well, I finally penetrated his disguise and with the aid of the sheriff and some others, notably an old colored man by the name of Eben Prescott, I again cleaned out his bunch. Then he and I had another race. I chased him into the Big Thicket north of Beaumont. Was closing in on him, but the trail through the Thicket led to the bank of a stream known as the Black Water. His horse fell down the bank and threw him into the stream. The Black Water is deadly infested with snakes and alligators, and the bed of the stream partakes of the nature of quicksand; anything caught in that mud is doomed. I never heard of anybody going into the Black Water and coming out alive, but Shaw evidently did. I watched for a while, but he never appeared above surface. I felt pretty sure he was done for, but I was not absolutely sure. I surmise he swam under water to a nearby bend in the stream, somehow dodged the snakes and the alligators and crawled out into the brush and made good his escape. To show up here!"

"To show up here?" repeated Medford.

"Yes, to show up here. *Loco Lobo is Tobar Shaw!*"

"You mean it?"

"I am convinced it is so," Slade answered. "Remember I kept saying that Lobo's mode of operation reminded me of somebody who employed similar methods? And, although I have never gotten a really good look at him, the set of his shoulders, his general build and his carriage struck a chord of memory, although I couldn't for the life of me recall of just whom he reminded me. Well, all of a sudden it came to me, just a little while ago. There is no doubt in my mind but that Loco Lobo and Tobar Shaw are one and the same. Which means we're up against what, I firmly believe, is the worst and smartest killer Texas ever produced."

"Which is saying plenty," snorted Medford.

"Yes, it is," Slade agreed. "The devil appears to get a sadistic pleasure from murder; he kills wantonly. Witness the shooting to pieces of the driver and guard of the Catarina Stage, and the needless killing of the Jimson Store manager, and other killings you've told me about. Tobar Shaw leaves no witnesses if he can help it. Or if he does leave one alive it is for a purpose, like the clerk of the Zapata bank, who gave an excellent description of his appearance as it is here, just what Shaw wanted him to do, as I mentioned to you before. So there is your Loco Lobo, as we might as well call him, and dropping a loop on him is going to be a real chore."

"Uh-huh, but I gather, you twice put him out of business and had him on the run," the sheriff observed. "I figure next time he ain't going to be able to run fast enough. Third time's the charm, they say."

"Hope you're right," Slade smiled.

"Hmmm!" the sheriff added, " 'Pears I rec'lect that all three times you tangled with him hereabouts you sent him skedaddling, and twice busted up his stealing for him, aside from giving quite a few of his hellions their comeuppance. Sounds like he's pretty darn smart, all right, and plumb bad, from your description, but my money's on *El Halcón.* Let us drink!"

Marie joined them and the subject was dropped for the time being.

Vocally, that is, for Slade's mind was plenty active, endeavoring to anticipate what Loco Lobo was contemplating. That the outlaw leader would strike soon he was convinced. It would be necessary for him to pull some chore to offset his recent reversals. His followers must be getting a mite jittery, and no head of a bunch can sustain his standing without producing results. Also, he

137

must be running somewhat short of hands, and did he hope to enlist recruits he'd have to show them it was worth their while to sign up with him.

"Drat!" Marie exclaimed. "Miguel is calling me to the back room for something." As she trotted off, the sheriff, who had evidently been turning something over in his mind, remarked, "Well, one thing's sure for certain, the hellion ain't going to steal any oil wells here."

Slade smiled. "Don't be too sure," he warned. "He may have something of that nature in mind."

"But there isn't any oil here," the sheriff protested.

"Not in sight," Slade admitted, "but unless I'm very much geologically wrong, it is just a matter of time until oil will be struck here and oil refining and shipping will play no small part in Laredo's industrial development. Some folks owning land hereabouts will end up millionaires."

"If you say it's so, I guess it is so," replied the sheriff. "Anyhow, I aim to hang onto a few acres I own up to the northeast, just in case."

"You'll be very wise to do so," Slade said. "Meanwhile we have a more pressing problem, what to do about the gentleman who at the moment is called Loco Lobo. His 'wheels seem very well oiled,' the way they've been turning over since he squatted here."

"And I'll be hanged if I know," Medford admitted frankly. "Let us drink!"

12

Marie came from the back room. "What's the matter?" she asked. "You two are as solemn and silent as a pair of owls. Why don't you say something?"

"We are giving the impression of wisdom we don't possess," Slade explained. "The owl, you know, has the reputation of being very wise, chiefly because he keeps a tight latigo on his jaw, while everybody thinks the parrot, really a much smarter bird, is terrapin-brained because he's all the time gabbin'."

"Intimating that the parrot and I are birds of a feather?" she retorted.

"Well, if you are adorned with feathers, I've failed to notice," he returned pointedly. Marie giggled and refrained from arguing the point.

While they had been talking, and thinking, the cantina had been filling up and was now well crowded. At the far end of the bar, a group of young Mexican *vaqueros* had their heads together; they kept casting glances toward the table Slade occupied. Finally one disengaged himself from the group and strolled across the room. He paused at the table, smiling and nodding.

"Capitan," he said insinuatingly, will you not do us the very great favor?"

"Be glad to," *El Halcón* replied. "What is it?"

"That *Capitan* sing for us, as he did once before," the *vaquero* said. He nodded toward the orchestra leader who was approaching, and holding out a guitar in a suggestive manner.

"Yes, Walt, please do," Marie broke in.

"All right, I can stand it if you can," Slade acceded. He took the guitar, followed the orchestra leader to the little raised platform that accommodated the musicians. All eyes turned toward him. Men nudged others to stop them talking. Silence fell.

Slade ran his fingers over the strings of the instrument with the crisp power that marks the born musician. He smiled at his waiting audience, threw back his black head, and sang.

He sang in a voice as deep and powerful as the flooded Rio Grande thundering in its sunken gorge, as melodious as the murmur of rain drops on the chaparral leaves and the whisper of the wind through the prairie grasses — a voice like to golden wine gushing into a crystal goblet. And as the great metallic baritone-bass soared and lilted and rolled its magic through the room, there was a cathedral-hush, and all activities ceased.

The trails run east and the trails run west,
By forest and dale and rill,
But O the lure of the winding trail
That vanishes over the hill!

Up there, blue-black against the sky,
Stands the changing edge of the world,
With its haunting lure and mystery
And its far-flung challenge hurled.

A thousand wondrous visions
Are lying just over the crest,
And ever the strange, unknown
Is the dream that's counted best.

By pine and purple heather,
By orchid and feathery palm
Down where the green waves thunder,
Through the desert's shimmering calm,

The trails go pouring onward,
But ever the strongest to thrill

Is the golden trail that vanishes
Over the distant crest of the hill!

The music ended in a crash of chords. For a moment the silence endured, then was shattered by a roar of applause, and shouts for another.

He sang another, a rollicking ballad of the range. Then, in deference to a number of rivermen present, some of them old, former deep-water sailors, he sang a booming ballad of the sea.

There were tears on Marie's dark lashes when he returned to the table.

"The trail that goes over the hill!" she said softly. "My rival!" The old sheriff smiled.

"It's getting so every night is payday night in this pueblo," he remarked sententiously. "Just listen at the hullabaloo, won't you! Don't the hellions ever sleep?"

"Oh, it isn't late, just the shank of the evening," Slade replied.

"A darn long shank," Medford grumbled. "Those clock hands are shoving around toward twelve mighty fast. Well, think I'll mosey up town for a while and look things over. Be seeing you."

It was Marie who, unwittingly, gave Slade the clue he needed.

"Oh, by the way," she remarked, "what

143

Uncle Tobe said about the clock hands reminds me of something. See those three men at the table over by the far corner of the dance floor? They've been there quite a while, and they keep watching the clock. As I passed by, I heard one of them say, 'Plenty of time; she doesn't leave till eleven-twenty-one.' Guess he meant twenty-one minutes past eleven o'clock, didn't he?"

"The chances are he did," Slade agreed.

"Wonder who he was talking about?" Marie went on. "None of the girls leave that early."

"Girls work in other places besides this one," Slade replied evasively.

"That's right," she admitted. "And some of the places aren't very fussy; if it's good for business, a girl can leave whenever she's of a mind to. Well, I have to get back on the floor — not enough girls to go around tonight, and I have to do something to earn my pay. Be with you after a while."

It was Slade's turn to glance at the clock. The hands stood at ten minutes to eleven, in railroad parlance, "ten-fifty." He turned his attention to the three men Marie had pointed out. They wore rangeland garb and gave every appearance of being cowhands. It was rather unusual for a puncher to employ the jargon of railroad men. His interest in the trio abruptly increased. For he knew very well they were not discussing a woman, as Marie thought.

Some years before, the advent of two railroads, one from Corpus Cristi, the other from Mexico, had put an end to Laredo's isolation and opened a large part of the Mexican markets to Texas. Now the Corpus Cristi road was doing a booming business. And Slade knew that a train for Corpus Cristi was due to leave the Santa Rita Avenue station at eleven-twenty-one.

Covertly, he studied the three men. They were quiet, alert-appearing individuals with keen eyes and hard mouths. Slade experienced a feeling that they didn't miss much of what went on around them. One glanced at the clock and their heads drew together in low-voiced conversation. A moment later they stood up and Slade noted that all three wore guns, and he was of the opinion that they didn't wear them as ornaments. He watched them saunter to the door. Obeying a sudden impulse, he waved to Marie and sauntered out also. He was just a mite curious about the trio who gave the appearance, he thought, of being somewhat out of the ordinary.

Reaching the street, at once he spotted his quarry walking at a leisurely pace toward

Santa Rita Avenue. He followed, keeping back far enough so that the three men were barely visible to the eyes of *El Halcón* — which meant that *he* was not at all visible to them. He saw them enter the railroad station and speeded up until he reached a point from where he could peer through a window; the three were at the ticket window buying tickets. He edged back in the shadow and waited. A few moments and the men came out of the station and entered the first coach behind the express car of the train that was just about ready to pull out. He waited again, until the conductor called "all aboard" and waved a high-ball to the engineer before mounting the front steps of the first coach.

The locomotive exhaust thundered; the train began moving; Slade sped forward, seized the rear grab irons of the last coach and swung aboard before the conductor or the breakman could get back to close the door. Leaning comfortably against the coach end wall, he rolled a cigarette and waited for the conductor to put in an appearance.

A little time passed, the conductor taking up tickets, and then that worthy, who knew *El Halcón* well, appeared.

"Why, hello, Mr. Slade!" he exclaimed.

"Where are you headed for?"

"John, I don't know for sure, yet," the Ranger replied. "Those three gents who entered the first coach, where are *they* headed for?"

"Rio Grande City," the con replied. "Something up?"

"I don't know for sure," Slade repeated. "I'm just sort of playing a hunch. Suppose your express car is packing considerable money tonight?"

"It sure is, a big shipment," the conductor answered, looking startled. "You think —"

"I don't just know what to think, but as I said, I'm playing a hunch; just got a notion it won't be a bad idea to keep an eye on them."

The conductor stared at him, his face worried. "Think I oughta sound 'em out a bit?" he asked.

"You stay away from them," Slade instantly vetoed the suggestion. "If my hunch happens to be a straight one and they surmised you were suspicious, your life would very likely not be worth a busted peso. Go about your business as usual, start working on your papers as you usually do on leaving Laredo. I'm going up ahead."

The conductor looked even more startled. "Okay, I'll do as you say," he agreed.

147

Slade sauntered through the coaches. The train was not overly crowded, but he noted a few oldtimers who might possibly be counted on to lend a hand if the going got too rough. He paused in the rear vestibule of the first coach, peered through the door glass.

There was only a scattering of passengers in the coach, most of them dozing. He instantly spotted the three individuals in question, seated near the front of the car; they appeared to be concentrating their attention on the starlit landscape flitting by the windows; they wore an air of expectancy. Looked very much like they were watching for certain landmarks. Slade's interest in them heightened. Now he was convinced that something was in the wind, very likely something reprehensible.

The train made a couple of stops. At each only a few passengers got on, occupying the rear coaches, and Slade was not disturbed.

After the second stop, Slade knew the train was passing over a rugged and sparsely settled area, and it seemed to him the air of expectancy worn by the three increased. He instinctively tensed for action.

Abruptly the men rose to their feet, glanced around, and walked rapidly to the front door. They opened it, passed through and closed it behind them. None of the dozing passengers paid them any attention. Slade waited a couple of minutes, then followed. When he reached the vestibule he saw the express door stood ajar — a door that should have been locked and probably had been — and had been opened by a key in the possession of one of the trio. He listened a moment, caught a mutter of voices. The door swung open noiselessly to his gentle push and he was inside the express car. Before his eyes was spread the tableau he expected.

13

The express messenger squatted beside the big iron safe, twirling the combination knob. And with good reason; the muzzle of a gun was pressed against the back of his neck. The other two robbers, guns in hand, one leaning against the car side door, watched the operation; their backs were to *El Halcón*.

The safe door swung open, and at the same instant, the crackling locomotive exhaust shut off, brake rigging jangled, and the shoes screamed against the wheels.

The express car jumped, bucked, careened wildly. The messenger was sprawled on the floor. The gun that had been pressed against the back of his neck boomed, the bullet slashing into the safe. The three robbers were hurled sideways and saw Slade, who had been slammed off balance and against the side wall. The car volcanoed gunfire.

Weaving, ducking, Slade answered the outlaws shot for shot. One slumped forward onto his face. Answering slugs ripped the Ranger's shirt sleeve, tore through the top of one boot, whisked his hat sideways on his head. A second man fell, screaming and writhing. The remaining robber lined sights, then fairly flew through the air as a thundering explosion blew the car door to pieces, the hurtling fragments smashing his body to pulp. Yellowish smoke billowed into the car.

Dazed, blinded, his ears ringing, Slade pawed at the side of the car for support, caught his balance and whirled to face the yawning black opening that had been a door. He shot instinctively as heads bobbed into view. There was a yelp of pain, a volley of profanity; the heads vanished. Bullets poured into the car, but Slade was snugged against the side wall and none found a mark. Reloading his guns with frantic speed, he watched the door for more heads.

But now the train had ground to a stop and more guns were cracking outside. The oldtimers in the first coach, getting the drift of things, joined in the fray.

A voice roared a command. There was a crashing of brush, then the beat of fast hoofs going away from there. Slade leaped to the door, saw four shadowy riders racing their horses across the prairie and emptied his guns after them, without results.

"Mr. Slade!" a voice was shouting. "Mr. Slade!"

"Okay," the Ranger called reply. "Everything under control. Come on in."

The conductor clambered through the door, panting. "You all right?" he gasped.

"Fine as frog hair," *El Halcón* answered as he again reloaded his guns.

The express messenger, who had also been knocked out by the explosion, was sitting up rubbing his bruised head and swearing with a fervor that relieved Slade of anxiety as to the extent of his injuries. The conductor glanced at the bodies strewn around.

"Well, you sure took care of the devils," he remarked.

"That stick of dynamite chucked against the car door took care of one," Slade replied. "He's something of a mess. Any more carcasses outside?"

"Nope, them three's all," the conductor replied.

"So all the outside bunch got in the clear including, I expect, the head of the pack," Slade observed disgustedly. "I'm begining to almost believe that hellion does bear a charmed life."

The messenger was on his feet. "Feller," he said to Slade, "you sure saved the company a passel of money tonight; that safe is jammed with it. And much obliged for saving me from getting my brains blowed out," he added, a trifle shakily. "I've a notion the devils wouldn't have left me alive." Slade thought he was probably right.

"What shape is your train in?" he asked the conductor.

"Not too bad," the con replied. "Pilot knocked off and the front end of the engine bunged up some. Nobody hurt much. Lucky that mess of rocks and crossties wasn't on a curve."

"Let's have a look," Slade suggested.

Together they approached the hissing locomotive. The front was considerably damaged and the front truck wheels rested on the ties.

"Rails spread," he said. "Will be something of a chore to put things in shape." He glanced back along the straight stretch of track.

"I think they miscalculated a little," he observed.

"Had no intention of wrecking the train, figuring their inside men would have everything under control."

"Which they would have if it wasn't for you," the conductor interpolated.

"Yes, I'm of the opinion they expected no

difficulty," the Ranger said. "Brought along a stick of dynamite for use in case of emergency. When they heard the shooting inside the car I guess they figured it was the time to use it — which was sort of unlucky for one of their bunch and possibly lucky for me; the devil had gotten over his scare and was lining sights."

"Doubt if it would have done him any good," said the conductor. "Lining sights with *El Halcón* is just a nice way to commit suicide."

The passengers crowded around Slade, praising him, congratulating him on the outcome of his ruckus with the robbers.

"The sort of a deputy Sheriff Medford has been needing for quite a while," one old-timer declared.

"You fellows came in handy with your gunplay at just the right moment," Slade told them. "Things were getting a mite hot."

"If the light had been a little better and we'd have gotten started sooner, we might have bagged the rest of the sidewinders," the oldtimer said. "By the time we really got into action, it was sorta long sixgun range."

Slade turned to the conductor. "You have a portable telegraph instrument aboard, don't you? Get it and I'll hook up the wires," glancing at the tall pole alongside the right-of-way. "You can send? If you can't, I can."

"I can tap out enough to tell 'em what happened," the conductor stated.

"Tell them to send an engine from Laredo to pull the train back out of the way, so the wrecker can get busy with this locomotive and the track. The passengers can be discharged at Laredo till things are cleaned up. Will be quicker than sending a wreck train from Corpus Cristi. Tell them if they can locate Sheriff Medford in a hurry to bring him along."

The instrument was procured. Slade ascended the tall telegraph pole with ease and hooked it up. When the conductor called okay, he loosened the extension wires, tossed them to the ground and slid down the pole.

"Say, you must have some squirrel blood in your veins, the way you went up that stick," the conductor remarked admiringly.

"An easy one to climb," Slade deprecated the feat.

"Uh-huh, for a squirrel," grunted the con. "By the way, the hogger always has a passel of sandwiches, a jug of coffee, and a bucket to heat it in his seatbox. What say we have a swig and a bite?"

"The best thing you've said yet," Slade agreed.

The engineer who, along with the fireman, had suffered but a few minor bruises, produced the edibles. The coffee was heated on a shovelful of glowing coals from the firebox and Slade joined them in a tasty snack.

After which, he browsed around in the brush and located the horses intended for the three outlaws. Once again he believed the brands were an East Texas burn but couldn't be sure. He removed the rigs and turned them loose to fend for themselves until picked up, tossed the saddles and bridles into the express car.

Less than an hour passed before the engine from Laredo arrived. With it came Sheriff Medford. He and Slade occupied an isolated seat in one of the coaches and talked on the way to town.

"Yes, a very smooth try, worthy of Tobar Shaw's acumen," Slade concluded, after briefing the sheriff on the details of the incident. "Nothing crude like really wrecking the train, possibly turning over the express car or having to shoot their way in. The plan, of course, was just to stop the train. Then the three inside men, having looted the safe, would drop off and the bunch would hightail before anybody but the messenger, very likely dead by that time, realized what was happening. I'd say the engineer was either going a mite faster than usual or was a bit slow in sighting the obstruction. Otherwise he wouldn't have slammed on his brakes under full air pressure as he did. One of the little things not even the brainiest outlaw could anticipate."

"Uh-huh, another *little thing* they didn't anticipate — *El Halcón* on the job," the sheriff interpolated dryly.

Slade smiled. "Well, anyhow, 'swiping the gage,' as a railroader would phrase it, caused the express car to do some lively jumping, which threw the three hellions off balance, to my advantage. To say nothing of very likely saving the messenger from getting a slug through his neck."

"I noticed you got one of the sidewinders through the neck," Medford observed. "The other one dead center. And the third one got made hash of by hunks of car door. All present and accounted for. Guess it happened in Zapata County, not Webb, but who the devil cares! Coroner can set on 'em in Laredo. Little thing like that don't matter, no-how."

"Little things, how tremendously important they can prove to be," Slade said musingly. "Just a few words Marie overheard and mentioned to me meant the difference between success and failure of a daring robbery attempt, and life or death, quite probably, for an innocent man. Makes one wonder."

"And makes one wonder how in blazes *El Halcón* always manages to interpret those *little things* correctly," said the sheriff.

"Training," Slade smiled. Medford snorted explosively.

The train rolled into Laredo. The passengers disembarked to seek solace at the various bars; it was still not very late for Laredo. With the track cleared, the wreck train boomed east to clean up the mess. The sheriff arranged to have the three bodies packed to his office, he and Slade preceding them.

Examination of the bodies was accompanied by the same wearisome monotony; nothing of significance was discovered, save money.

"Anyhow, the county treasury is getting rich," Medford said cheerfully. "And I've a notion *amigo* Loco Lobo is getting sorta 'poor' as to hired hands."

"Yes, I've a notion he's scraping the bottom of the barrel," Slade agreed. "But he's still running loose, and that's the important thing."

"Can't dodge the loop forever," predicted the sheriff. "Just a matter of time."

However, when people started dropping in to view the bodies, business picked up a mite. Several recalled seeing the trio hanging around the riverfront. One bar owner said they had been in his place a number of times, always together, never mixed with the other patrons to amount to anything, would drop out of sight every now and then for several days and then show up with plenty of money, although they never appeared to work.

"Yes, Lobo is picking up recruits from the kind that are to be found everywhere along the river," Slade said, after the informant had departed. "Those three are typical brush poppers, ruthless, not overly intelligent, but capable. The sort that will carry out orders given them by somebody who can plan and direct. Do very well so long as they don't have to think for themselves. I've contacted that brand more than once and usually they sooner or later make a wrong move. May happen in this case, which would work to our advantage. Well, suppose we shut up shop and call it a night; it is getting a bit late, now. I'm heading for Miguel's cantina."

"I'll go along," said the sheriff. "All this excitement makes me hungry, thirsty, too."

Late though it was, the cantina was still doing plenty of business. Heads turned as they entered, hands were waved. The word of the thwarted robbery had gotten around and everybody was discussing it.

Marie joined them and regarded Slade resignedly. "Oh, I suppose I'm getting used to it," she said. "When you didn't come back right away, I knew you were mixed up in something, but I felt you'd come through all right, as usual. Suppose you tell me all about it."

Medford who had been well briefed by the conductor, the express messenger, and the passengers, proceeded to do so. Marie sighed and shook her head.

"A woman who takes up with him is, how would you say it, Uncle Tobe, terrapin-brained? Yes, I guess that's it. But," she added with her flashing smile, "it's worth it."

The sheriff ordered a meal and a snort. Slade settled for coffee. Marie glanced at the clock and trotted off to the dressing room to change her costume.

"I can't get over the slick way those hellions planned that robbery," Medford remarked reflectively, between bites. "They sure knew their business."

"I'm pretty sure the one Marie overheard was a former railroader," Slade replied. "He knew all the angles, including what type of key needed to open the end door of the express car. He was the one least affected when the engineer slammed on his brakes and might have given me my comeuppance had he not made the mistake of being against the side door of the car when the dynamite cut loose."

"Yep, quite a mistake," Medford agreed. "Got himself blown full of splinters.

"Well," he added a little later, "I've finished my surrounding and here comes your gal all dressed up and looking mighty cute. Guess we might as well call it a night."

After his breakfast, around mid morning, Slade wandered about the town for a while, hoping to encounter something interesting, with negative results. Everything appeared peaceful, citizens going about their various businesses cheerfully, pausing for a drink or to chat on street corners. Too darn peaceful, he feared, for he was experiencing an uneasy premonition that something was due to happen. Finally he gave over his quest and headed for the sheriff's office. As he neared it, he saw a man coming from the other direction, on the run. He held something in his hand and whisked into the office. Slade quickened his pace.

14

Since the robbery and the double murder on their premises, the Zapata bank officials had taken added precautions. There was an armed guard on the floor outside the grilled partition at all times who vigilantly scrutinized strangers entering the building.

But there certainly appeared nothing alarming about the tall, neatly dressed, commonplace-looking man who entered, carrying a packet of bills in his hand. His face was devoid of outstanding features. He gave the impression of a prosperous businessman.

Just the same, the guard moved close to him and slightly behind as he approached the manager's window. It was lunch time and only the guard and the manager were in the bank at the moment.

The manager's attention focused on the sheaf of large denomination bills the stranger carried in plain view, which was what was intended.

"I would like to open an account and make a deposit," the stranger said in a pleasantly modulated voice. "I plan to purchase land from the irrigation people and prefer to make my payments by check."

"Certainly, sir, be glad to accommodate," replied the manager, reaching for the bills. "Your name, sir?"

At that moment there was a clatter of hoofs outside and voices raised in altercation. Two riders, one from the west, the other from the east, jerked their mounts to a halt facing each other and began bellowing curses and threats.

The guard, not unnaturally, turned to glance out the window. He died, a knife in his back, the point puncturing his heart. In the same bewildering flicker of motion, the "depositor" whirled to face the manager, who stared into a gun muzzle. The gunman spoke a single word, his voice abruptly harsh and menacing, "Open!" He nodded toward the grilled door.

The trembling manager obeyed. The gun wielder stepped in, whisked a canvas sack from beneath his coat, gestured to the open vault.

"Fill it up, everything," he ordered.

The now thoroughly terrified manager did

as he was told. The other seized the sack, jerked a pucker string tight.

"Better stay right where you are for a while," he said and strode to the back door, which opened onto an alley. He turned the key which was in the lock, opened the door and stepped out, closing it behind him. The manager, literally frozen with fright, heard hoofs clatter, fading into the distance. At the same moment, one of the vituperating horsemen in the street whirled his cayuse and raced west, the other thundering behind him, still shouting threats. The whole episode had taken little more than two minutes.

The manager stayed right where he was for several moments, against the chance the killer might return, then ran to the street, calling for help. He was incoherent from his harrowing experience and it was some little time before he could make people understand what had happened.

The sheriff was sent for and arrived shortly.

"What did the sidewinder look like, Bert?" he asked the manager.

"Mac, I hardly know," the official replied. "I didn't get much more'n a glimpse of him. All I really noticed was that he was tall and his eyes looking at me over gunsights were bad, plumb bad."

"Eyes have a habit of looking that way, over gunsights," Sheriff McArdle observed dryly. "Gunsights seem to do things to 'em."

All anybody could remember anent the two horsemen who staged the phony ruckus in front of the bank was that they looked like cowhands.

Before embarking on a fruitless chase of the robbers, McArdle sent a wire to Sheriff Medford at Laredo, informing him that it appeared the robbers were headed his way.

Medford was swearing over the Zapata sheriff's message when Slade entered the office. He handed it to the Ranger, who glanced at the contents, passed it back, and sat down and began rolling a cigarette.

"Loco Lobo again," he said, when the brain tablet was finished and lighted. "Yes, no doubt of it. That job had the Tobar Shaw touch; smooth as goose grease we'll learn when we get the details I'm willing to bet." He glanced at the telegram again.

"Do not know what they looked like," was McArdle's final statement.

"Yes, Loco Lobo, minus his disguise," he said.

"And what the devil are we going to do about it?" demanded the sheriff.

Slade was silent until he'd smoked his

cigarette to a short butt, which he carefully pinched out, then he said, "Tobe," he said, "what is the last thing you'd figure Lobo to do?"

"I'm hanged if I know," Medford replied wearily. "Maybe he'll drop in here and squat for a gab, with neither of us recognizing him. He seems to have the nerve to do anything, and able to get by with anything. What do you think?"

"I believe," Slade answered slowly, "that the last thing he'd figure us to think of is that hangout, the old cabin up in the brush country, where we intercepted Si Brenner's herd of stolen cows. I'm playing a hunch that he'll head for that cabin and lie low for a day or two and divide the loot. I'll admit it's a sort of loco-sounding hunch, but somehow I can't help but feel it could well be a straight one."

"Well, judging from past performance of your blasted hunches, I'd say it's worth giving a whirl," said Medford. "When do we start?"

"Not until shortly after dark," Slade decided. "Against the unlikely possibility that there may be someone in town keeping tabs on us. There might be such a thing as a short cut to that clearing we don't know about, though I doubt it. Anyhow, we have plenty of time. Loco and his devils will have a long ride, if they do head for the hangout. They will have to bypass the irrigation works and circle around to the north. Hunt up your deputies and tell them what's in the wind, to be here, ready to ride, an hour after sunset. Pack along the bulls-eye lantern, Tobe, it's going to be a very dark night; sky's overcast."

The afternoon wore on. Slade and the sheriff ate an early dinner at the Montezuma and returned to the office. The deputies were there waiting. After a smoke they started.

Outside of town, Slade paused long enough to make sure they were not followed, then gave the order to proceed. At a good pace they rode west and north on the river trail.

Without difficulty, Slade located the opening in the brush that was the old Indian track running north to the rangeland. A mile or so from its mouth, where the ground was soft, he called a halt.

"Light the lantern," he told Medford. "I want to have a look."

On hands and knees he examined the surface of the trail, by the light of the lantern, closed the slide, and stood up.

"Hunch is a straight one, so far," he announced. "Horses have passed this way only a few hours back, headed north. Well, here goes. Keep your eyes and ears open at the bends; we take it slow and easy now."

He was more than usually vigilant as they rode the crooked track, but nothing happened and after a while he knew they were nearing the clearing. A little more slow progress and he said, his voice little above a whisper, "Here we leave the horses, in the brush. I don't think there is a reception committee awaiting our arrival, but we'll conduct ourselves as if there were."

"You're darn right," Medford breathed. "There's no telling what that horned toad will do."

The horses, except Shadow, were tethered in the brush and told to keep quiet; the posse stole forward on foot, reaching the edge of the clearing without mishap.

The night was very dark, but there was enough cloud-filtered starshine for them to perceive the shadowy outlines of the old cabin. No light was visible. No sound broke the stillness.

"Think they're in there waiting for us?" Medford breathed.

"I doubt it," Slade replied; "but we've got to make sure."

"How about crashing the door, fast?"

"Would be rank foolishness," Slade instantly vetoed the suggestion. "If there really happens to be somebody in there, waiting, we'd be settin' quail when the door opened."

"Guess that's so," Medford admitted. After which there was silence while Slade studied the dimly seen building. He didn't like the situation at all. If the outlaws had headed for the cabin, they would surely have arrived before now. Of course, his conclusion could have been wrong and their destination elsewhere, but he still did not believe it was. But to all indications the cabin was without occupancy. And yet, as he gazed, the old shack seemed to exude a nameless threat, some uncanny menace, the nature of which he could not divine but which he felt was very real.

In men who ride much alone with danger as a constant stirrup companion, there develops a subtle sixth sense that warns of peril when none, apparently, exists, and in *El Halcón* that sense was strongly developed indeed. And now the voiceless monitor was setting up a clamor in his brain. Somewhere a nightjar was sounding, and the little insect's monotonous plaint seemed to shape into words, "Stay back! Stay back! Stay back!"

Just a figment of too lively an imagination, of course, but the monitor in his brain seemed to take up the warning, "Stay back! Stay back!" Oh, the devil! He had to learn if there was anybody in the building, that was all there was to it.

"Tobe," he whispered, "hand me the lantern. It's lighted? Okay, keep the slide closed."

"What you going to do?" the sheriff asked apprehensively.

"I'm going to try and get a peek through that window," the Ranger replied.

"Crossing that clearing will be taking one helluva chance," the sheriff protested.

"Not too much," Slade replied. "Dark as it is, I don't think I will be spotted through that dirty window. Anyhow, here goes!"

And as he left the shelter of the growth, the nightjar's metallic plaint seemed to change to, "Come back! Come back!"

The sheriff held his breath as Slade glided across the open space.

"Made it!" he whispered a moment later. "He's against the wall."

Slade had reached the cabin wall and stood with his ear pressed against the logs. For a long moment he stood motionless, and heard nothing; he decided to take a chance. Setting the bull's eye of the lantern against the window pane he flipped the slide. The beam illumined the interior dimly, but enough for him to see the single room was untenanted.

But it also showed something Slade instantly felt was out of order. The table had been upended and to one of its legs something was attached. He shifted the beam a trifle, got a better look, and whistled under his breath. Snapping the slide shut, he turned and sped back to his companions.

"They've been here, all right, and have left a nice little reception committee to welcome us," he said. "The cunning devil, familiar with the way I work, figured I would surmise just what I did — that he'd make for the hangout and we'd attempt to intercept him. So he turned the table upside down and fastened a sawed-off shotgun to one of the legs, evidently trained on the door by a string secured from the trigger to the door knob and all set to blow from under his hat anybody who attempted to open it."

"And that somebody would have been you, as he knows darn well, the blankety-blank-blank!" swore Medford. "What are we going to do?"

"I want to get a look inside that cabin," Slade said. "May be some clue in there as to his next move. Remember the plat of the irrigation project we found in the pocket of that drygulcher. That saved the irrigation's payroll."

"How about going through the window?" Medford hazarded.

"Too narrow," Slade replied. "That's out. Let me think a minute."

His gaze roved over the clearing. The cloud bank was thinning a little, the starlight brighter.

"I believe I've got it," he said a moment later. "See those tall saplings over there to the left? We should be able to fell one of those without much trouble. That will give us a nice long pole. We can stay back at one end and ram the door open with it. I'm afraid to risk trying to stand at one side, turn the knob and fling the door open. Might not get my arm back in time, with it opening inward as it does. But with the pole we should be safe enough."

"Sounds good to me," said the sheriff. "Let's go."

After considerable hacking with heavy clasp knives, they managed to bring down the sapling Slade selected. Trimming off the branches, they had a stout pole nearly thirty feet long.

"This should do it," *El Halcón* said. "All

back at this end. We'll hit the door a slanting blow and that way be out of line. All set? Hit it!"

All hands gripping the butt of the pole firmly, they rushed forward. The far end of the makeshift battering ram struck the door a resounding blow and crashed it wide open.

There was a deafening roar. The posse was knocked sprawling by the concussion. The whole front of the cabin flew to pieces. Chunks of timber and chinking rained all about them, but miraculously nobody was struck.

15

Slade was on his feet before the echoes of the explosion had ceased slamming back and forth.

"Get going!" he shouted. "Get going! That shack's on fire and the clearing will be bright as day. Get going!"

"What in blazes happened?" panted the sheriff as they beat a hurried retreat to the brush. "I thought the sky had done fallen down."

"I was wrong," Slade replied. "I thought that shotgun was trained on the door, but it wasn't. It was trained on a bundle of dynamite lying beside the door. A real nice try, that one."

"And if it wasn't for you and we'd tried to open that door standing alongside it, we'd be under that blazin' mess, and I don't hanker to burn before my time," gulped Medford. "Walt, that scoundrel ain't a man, he's a devil."

"At least a fair simulacrum of one," Slade conceded as they snugged down in the brush. "Outsmarted again, that's all; the sidewinder is always a jump ahead of me," he added bitterly. "Keep your voices down. I doubt if they were hanging around somewhere waiting for the blast and aiming to slip back for a look at their handiwork, but we can't afford to take chances with Lobo; he's capable of anything. Everybody quiet now, and let me listen. We could get a chance to turn the tables on him, yet." He strained his ears to catch any sound of approach.

But only the crackle of the flames broke the silence. Finally Slade gave up in disgust.

"We might as well admit we're licked and go home," he said. "Nothing more we can do here. Just the same, stretch your ears and keep your eyes skinned against the chance that brainy gent may have lined up another little surprise for us."

However, either Loco Lobo had been confident the posse would be blown to smithereens or had run out of ideas, for they reached the river trail without incident.

Walt Slade was in a disgruntled mood as they headed for Laredo, feeling as he did that the elusive Tobar Shaw had, in the vernacular, put another one over on him.

The sheriff and the deputies, recalling how his wit saved them all from destruction, held otherwise and were loud in their praise.

"Nice of you to feel that way," *El Halcón* said, "but I still consider I was neatly outsmarted. Oh, well! Maybe next time."

When they reached the office, they found that Sheriff McArdle of Zapata County, after combing the prairie and the brush country with negative results, had decided to spend the night at Laredo, and was awaiting them. He filled in the details of the bank robbery.

"Loco Lobo, all right," Slade observed after McArdle departed in search of something to eat. "The Shaw touch. Staged the phony row in front of the bank to distract the guard's attention for the moment he needed to knife him. Knew the manager would concentrate on the money he carried and afterward would be too frightened to be able to give anything like a recognizable description of him."

"Wonder why he didn't kill the manager, too?" remarked Medford.

"Because he did not wish the sound of a shot to attract attention to the bank," Slade replied. "Oh, he never misses a bet and always knows exactly, beforehand, what moves to make. Undoubtedly one of his men had been studying the bank and its methods of operation, where the back door was set, for instance, what was lunch time, for the clerks, and so forth. When Shaw was ready to make his move, he had all the necessary details at his fingertips. He is utterly snake-blooded, with him murder is a pasttime."

Slade paused to roll and light a cigarette, then resumed: "As I said before, he is the most shadowy, most elusive character I ever met up with. Tobe, if he walked in here right now and sat down, I couldn't do a thing about it, for I have absolutely nothing on him that would stand up in court. When I chased him across the Tucumcari Desert, although convinced in my own mind that the man I pursued was Tobar Shaw, I couldn't prove it, for I never got close enough to him to be able to swear that my quarry was Tobar Shaw.

"The same applies to my contacts with him in Beaumont, where he was known as Turner Shane. I never saw him without his disguise — heavy black whiskers, thick-lensed glasses — a quite different appearing individual from Tobar Shaw of the Panhandle, nor did anybody else. Positive as I am that the man I followed through the Big Thicket, who fell into the Black Water, was

Tobar Shaw, again I could not prove it to the satisfaction of a jury. A good lawyer would make mincemeat of me.

"So that's how the situation stands. Once again I am convinced, convinced that Loco Lobo and Tobar Shaw are one and the same, and once again, I can't prove it, yet. I've just got to get the hellion dead to rights."

"Or right in line with your gun muzzle," grunted the sheriff.

"One or the other, I suppose," Slade smiled. "Neither will be easy. Frankly, I don't believe I've ever had such an opponent as Tobar Shaw. He is unique. Veck Sosna and Juan Covelo were vicious, cruel, deadly, but their methods were forthright; one could to an extent at least anticipate what they were contemplating. But it is almost impossible to track Shaw's devious reasoning; he just naturally doesn't fall into a pattern. Doesn't do what he is supposed to, and does do what no one would suspect.

"Take the second robbery of the Zapata bank. Who would dream the hellion would hit that bank again so soon, minus the disguise that is his trade mark, an entirely different person in every way, with an entirely different approach."

"That little chore of dynamitin' he tried

to pull off was sorta original, too," commented the sheriff.

"Yes, it was," Slade agreed. "That required some shrewd thinking on his part."

"Uh-huh, but it just happened that you outthought the devil," said Medford. "How you did it I don't know."

"I think the answer is that I am always a mite suspicious of the obvious," Slade replied. "That darn shack looked too innocent to be real. Even after I saw the shotgun wired to the table leg, I still couldn't believe Shaw would resort to an old trick like that. I firmly believe he anticipated that I'd get a look through the window and spot the thing. And if so, I'd know very well I could manage to push the door open, discharge the gun and still be in the clear. I was confident there was some sort of a catch involved, although I hadn't the slightest idea what it could be. Anyhow, I decided that getting too close to that door might not be healthy."

"Thank Pete you did," said Medford. "If I'd been in your place I'd have turned the knob and poked the door open with a stick or something, and got blown clean to glory. Well, it's getting sort of late. Don't you think we'd better amble down to Miguel's cantina and let the folks know you're okay?

Then to bed; I feel a mite tuckered."

"Not a bad idea," Slade agreed.

"Just the same I'll bet that horned toad is fit to be hog-tied, or will be when he learns you slipped outa his noose," Medford predicted as they made their way to the cantina.

"And don't bother your pretty head about this young hellion," he told Marie, after recounting the misadventure in the clearing. "He's always a jump ahead of the devils."

"I suppose so," she replied. "But he sure keeps me jumping out of my skin. Well, you must both be starved, yes!"

"I've a notion I can manage to choke down a bite," the sheriff admitted.

"And I'll make a try at it, too," Slade promised. "Here comes Miguel with his bottles, as usual."

"Miguel has exactly the right notion," Medford applauded. "Fill 'em up, Mig!"

Marie glanced at the clock. "And while you're eating, I'll change my dress," she said. "It's nearly closing time."

16

The following day, Slade again wandered about town, hoping to hit on some clue as to what would be Loco Lobo's next move. Of course there was a chance, after the good haul he made, that he would lie low for a while — which was of course what everybody would expect him to do. But Loco Lobo made a point of not conforming to the general viewpoint. It was more likely, Slade thought, that he would be active with little delay.

However, as the day wore on, he learned nothing he considered significant; if the outlaw wasn't lying low for a change, he was certainly keeping under cover.

Slade believed he would recognize Shaw without his Loco Lobo disguise, although it was quite probable that the cunning devil would figure some other way to change his appearance; that Slade was forced to admit.

He studied backs. Tobar Shaw had an

unusually straight back, and the set of his shoulders was a trifle peculiar. Slade believed he would spot that back anywhere. However, although there were plenty of straight backs around, none seemed to fill the bill. He chuckled, for despite the gravity of the situation in general, the quest struck a humorous note. Endeavoring to recognize a man by his back! Well, it was about all he had to go on.

The night that followed was equally barren of results. The next morning he was up fairly early and walked slowly down Convent Avenue and ascended the soaring arch of the International Bridge. Midway up the span he leaned against the rail and gazed southward.

A feathery mist hid the river and its banks, but quickly it was shot with silver and sapphire-blue, dissolved by slow enchantment until the shimmering water lay revealed, the high banks pink tourmaline and ruby in the rays of the sun. The day before the river had been almost at flood stage, but during the night it had fallen rapidly and was still falling, leaving a gleaming floor for the light to dance. Alert little birds darted here and there with incredible swiftness, leaving tiny footprints across the ribs and furrows of the wet sand. Slade marveled at the sudden brilliance of his surroundings as the sun climbed higher. And despite his somewhat morose frame of mind, he was uplifted by the feast of beauty spread before his eyes.

Yes, a beautiful land, well worth striving and fighting for. He walked on to that other land across the stately River of the Palms, where good men were also fighting for justice and decency.

Abruptly he quickened his pace; he was experiencing a presentiment that in Nuevo Laredo he might strike paydirt.

But as he wandered about the Mexican town with no results, he began to feel that he had been unduly optimistic. He stopped at several places, in some of which he was known, paused for some little time at Felipe's cantina to chat with Felipe and his bartenders. He was about to recross the river when, obeying a sudden impulse, he turned his steps toward the dubious saloon in which he had met Loco Lobo face to face and shot the gun from his hand.

There were but a few patrons present when he entered, for it was not quite noon, most of them rivermen he concluded. The moon-faced owner recognized him at once and came hurrying to greet him, wearing a broad smile. He had shrewd, twinkly little eyes set in rolls of fat, and a button nose. Slade rather liked his looks.

"*Capitan!*" he exclaimed. "You are welcome, most welcome. I am honored that again *El Halcón,* the good, the just, sees fit to visit my humble establishment. Come, *Capitan,* we will have the glass of wine together."

Smiling and bobbing, he led the way to a table in a far corner of the room, well away from the bar and the scattering of customers, motioned a waiter who brought the wine and retired. Still smiling, he raised his glass in salute. Then he glanced around and lowered his voice.

"*Capitan,*" he said. "I am glad, most glad you came today. It is fate! For I have something I think you should hear. Your friends, the *vaqueros,* who are also my *amigos,* tell me that you seek that one most evil who is known as *El Loco Lobo. Si?*"

"Has he been back since the other night?" Slade countered. The owner shook his head.

"He has not," he replied, "but some of those with whom he spoke have been. There were three here last night, men not good to look upon. Quite different from the pleasant *ladrones* who sojourn here at times, who but filch purses and steal all that is not nailed down. They made me think of the

185

snake that without warning strikes, those three. Two came in and sat at that table near the back room door. They appeared to be waiting. A third entered and joined them. They spoke together, their voices very low. I tried to overhear what was said, for I was sure it boded no good for somebody, possibly myself. But hear I could not until the one who entered last raised his voice a little."

"What did he say?" Slade asked.

"*Capitan,* these are the words," the owner answered. " 'Understand? Tomorrow, the crossing.' I would think he meant the old Indian Crossing from Laredo, *si?* Does it mean aught to you, *Capitan?*"

"Frankly, I don't know," Slade replied. "Sounds like a get-together of some sort. But at the Indian Crossing, that's a puzzler. That was all you heard?"

"That was all. The one who spoke departed at once, the others soon afterward, and glad was I to see them go."

For some moments Slade sat silent, studying his table companion, although not seeming to do so. He believed the man was sincere. The setting of a trap? Illogical to think so, under the circumstances. Unless the cantina owner was possessed of the second sight to the Nth degree, which was

186

decidedly unlikely, he could not have known that he, Slade, intended to visit his establishment; Slade didn't know it himself twenty minutes earlier. It was reasonable to think he would be anxious to please the *vaqueros,* the main asset of his business, in any way possible — to say nothing of what he well knew would very likely happen to him personally did those wild horsemen learn, or even suspect, he had double-crossed *El Halcón.*

Yes, his story rang true; but what the devil did it mean? Of course, it could possibly mean but a rendezvous with others fording the river from one bank to the other, doing so perhaps to avoid being spotted crossing by way of the International Bridge. But he felt that was not the answer.

"I repeat, I don't know what it means," he said. "But it could be important. *Gracias* for telling me."

"It is the pleasure to favor *El Halcón* in any way," the other instantly responded. "Let us drink!"

They proceeded to do so. After which Slade crossed the river to Laredo. As a precaution, he contacted Pancho Garza, at Miguel's cantina, and asked his opinion.

"I think the hombre spoke truth," the knife man said. "I know him; he is not bad.

187

As I said that night, *ladrones* from both sides of the river frequent his place, petty thieves with no great harm in them. Because of which he would be reluctant to contact the authorities, but would feel safe in confiding in *El Halcón*. Tonight, I and my *amigos* will keep a watch on that crossing and inform *El Capitan* do we note anything we think he should know about."

Slade thanked Pancho and then made his way to Bruni Street, by way of thence to the river, where he stood gazing toward the Indian Crossing slightly to the north. He studied the long ripple that marked the course of the underwater ledge from bank to bank. With the river at its present height and still falling, by night it would be possible for horsemen who knew the way to ford the river.

Suddenly he uttered a sharp exclamation. With his mind's eye he was seeing another ripple that extended from bank to bank of the Rio Grande. Which undoubtedly marked another and probably even more negotiable crossing — directly opposite where the old Indian track emptied onto the river trail.

"Yes, that could be the answer," he muttered aloud. "But what are the devils up to? Another widelooping? Could be." Turning, he hurried to Shadow's stable and got the rig on the big black.

But before mounting, he did some hard and fast thinking. From the point in question, the trail ran straight, in both directions, for a considerable distance, and at the mouth of the track northward through the brush was the crest of a slight rise. Did he go riding up the river trail, he stood an excellent chance of being spotted by anybody who might be holed up there, with very likely unpleasant results for himself. That course was definitely out.

He knew, however, that south of the Rio Grande, in Mexico, was another trail paralleling the course of the river, an old *Camino Real,* or Royal Road, although there wasn't much royal about it now, and it was very little traveled. By way of that he could reach a point from which he could see across the river to where the Indian track joined with the river trail in Texas. What would he do when he got there? He hadn't the slightest notion; just have to await developments, if any.

Crossing the bridge, he reached the trail without difficulty and rode at a fast pace, for he had no idea how much time he had or didn't have.

"Anyhow, it's a nice day for a ride and your legs need a mite of stretching, so june along, horse, and don't complain," he told Shadow, who snorted cheerful agreement and proceeded to do some leg stretching that flowed back the miles under his speeding irons.

The trail ran rather farther back from the river than did the one on the north shore, and there was a thick stand of brush on the river side. But now and then Slade could catch glimpses of the opposite shore and spot certain landmarks. Finally, with the sun low in the west, he knew he must be drawing close to his destination. He had been very alert in the course of the ride and now his vigilance increased and he slowed Shadow's pace, scanning the terrain ahead, watching for the opening in the brush he felt sure existed. He slowed still more, although the monitor in his brain seemed to be urging, *"Hurry! Hurry!"*

A few more tense moments and he spied the opening, fairly wide, flanked by tall brush. A quick glance at the ground showed him that cattle had passed that way no great while before — very likely some of the cows widelooped in recent weeks by Loco Lobo. He entered the opening, every nerve strung for instant action; no telling what he might meet along that winding path. He covered a couple of hundred yards and rode into an open space with the river bank but a short distance ahead. He glanced across the stream, here some five hundred yards in width, whipped from the saddle, sliding his heavy Winchester from the boot in the same ripple of movement. He knew he was within plain view from across the river, but he also knew he hadn't a moment to spare. His amazingly keen eyes had seen, at the edge of the growth where the old Indian track joined the river trail, the quick gleam of sunlight reflected from shifted metal.

And lumbering up the rise, almost to the crest, was a big coach drawn by six horses, the driver and a guard perched on the high seat. He knew it to be the Eagle Pass stage making its two-day trip to Laredo. And *El Halcón* understood. His voice rang out — "Back, Shadow, back!"

17

The big horse whirled and streaked into the growth. Slade clamped the rifle to his shoulder and sent a slug crashing through the brush directly above where he had spotted that telltale gleam of metal, purposely holding high the first shot. He followed it with another and another, lower down.

The result was instantaneous. Fire flickered from the chaparral. Lead stormed about him. Weaving, ducking, shifting, he continued to shoot. From the corner of his eye he saw the stage had halted at the lip of the crest, the driver and the guard leaping to the ground. The latter, realizing what was in the wind, began blazing away with his rifle.

Constantly on the move, Slade fired as fast as he could pull trigger, streaming bullets at his unseen target. The intrepid guard ran forward a couple of steps; his rifle smoked.

A riderless horse dashed from the growth

and pounded down the trail. A slug hit Slade's boot heel and nearly knocked him off his feet. Another whispered in his ear. Lowering his sights a trifle, he emptied the magazine.

A second horse burst into view and high-tailed after the first. As he reloaded with frantic speed, Slade realized no more lead was coming his way. He sent a few more shots into the growth for good measure, and kept moving.

The guard was waving a reassuring hand. Slade's great voice rolled in thunder across the water —

"Stay close to the brush!"

Guard and driver obeyed the order, hugging the chaparral. Slade, his eyes never leaving the distant bristle, waited a moment longer. He knew that fording the river he would be a settin' quail for anybody still holed up in the growth but decided to risk it. He whistled Shadow, mounted, his eyes still fixed on the far side of the river, put the big black to the water. Shadow thrust forth a tentative hoof, realized there was firm rock beneath it, and stepped out briskly. Slade held the Winchester ready for instant action. Looked like the remaining outlaws, if there had been more than two — and he was pretty well convinced there were

— had skalleyhooted back up the track. But he breathed relief when he reached the Texas shore and Shadow snorted his way onto dry land.

The guard left his shelter and came running to greet him, whooping with excitement. Slade saw he was a freckle-faced young fellow with a ready smile and gay, reckless blue eyes. The sort the stage people always tried to hire to guard their equipages.

"Feller, how in blazes did you happen along at just the right time?" he shouted. "If it wasn't for you, those sidewinders would have done us in, sure for certain. Much obliged for keepin' all the gals in Laredo and Eagle Pass from feelin' sad!" He roared with laughter. "Where *did* you come from?"

"Saw those gents holed up in the brush, waiting, and thought I'd better horn in," Slade explained evasively. The guard shook his carroty-red head.

"What kind of eyes you got, anyhow?" he marveled. "Saw 'em all the way across the river! We were right on top of them and didn't see 'em."

"The angle from where you were was bad," Slade replied smilingly.

The driver, a blocky oldtimer, spoke up. "Say, weren't you in Laredo last year? One of Tobe Medford's deputies?"

"Something of the sort," Slade admitted.

"Uh-huh, thought I remembered you," said the driver. "You did a darn good chore then, and it looks like you're still doin' 'em. Well, if Tobe takes a notion to retire when his term's up, as he's always talkin' about, you're my candidate for sheriff."

"I trust he will be in office for a long time yet," Slade replied. "He's a good man."

"Anyhow, he sure knows how to pick deputies," the driver declared. Slade changed the subject.

"Suppose we browse around and see what we bagged," he suggested. "Careful, now, one of that brand only wounded is dangerous as a broken-back rattler."

Cautiously, they entered the growth and quickly came upon two dead men sprawled on the ground. They were tough looking customers, but otherwise there was nothing outstanding about them. Slade was not the least surprised that neither was Loco Lobo. He was pretty sure it was Lobo fired the last shot that missed him by less than an inch. He examined the surface of the trail.

"Appears three horses went up it, fast," he said, "Well, guess we might as well shove these two into the coach and pack them to town with us. See you have no passengers today."

"Last two got off at Catarina," said the driver. "Nobody for Laredo today. By the way, I'm Nate Quigley. This young hellion hidin' behind the grin is Ben Manners. I seem to have sorta forgot your handle."

Slade supplied it and they shook hands.

"Nope, no passengers for Laredo today," the driver repeated, adding significantly, "but there's a box in that coach that's packin' plenty for Laredo. The company will have something to say to you, son, and they'll do more than just talk."

The bodies were placed in the coach, alongside a big iron strongbox, the doors locked.

"Figure maybe it was that blasted Loco Lobo and some of his bunch?" the driver asked as he mounted to his perch.

"I presume so," Slade answered. "Had all the earmarks of one of his chores."

"A pity he didn't catch one of those slugs," growled the driver. "But his time'll come, his time'll come."

Slade constantly scanned their surroundings and the terrain ahead as the stage resumed its interrupted journey, for although he did not really expect an encore, it was best not to take chances.

A couple of miles down the trail they came upon the two horses that, having recovered from their fright, were trying to graze. Slade removed the rigs and left the critters for somebody to pick up. The brands they bore were unfamiliar.

The stage rolled on, Shadow pacing beside it, and arrived safely at Laredo a little after dark. The bodies were deposited in the sheriff's office. Medford, who was present and wondering what had become of Slade, was too astounded to even swear intelligently. Quigley and Manners paused long enough to give a vivid account of what happened, then continued to the stage company's offices after again shaking hands with Slade, who sat down and rolled a cigarette. He felt that he had taken a trick this time, even though the arch-villain of the piece, as usual, escaped.

"Now suppose you start at the beginning and tell me how you managed it," Medford said. Slade proceeded to do so. The sheriff voiced a few weary remarks not meant for Sunday school.

"It's everlastingly beyond my understanding how you figure things out," he concluded.

"Well, once again the thing was fairly obvious," the Ranger replied. "Thanks to that chubby cantina owner's keen ears and quick mind — with quite a dash of luck added.

When I crossed the bridge, I hadn't the slightest intention of visiting his place. The notion came to me all of a sudden, out of a clear sky, as it were. And once again the Hand of Destiny, working in its inscrutable fashion to achieve its ends. Well, from the sublime to the ridiculous, as the saying goes, I'm hungry. Suppose we go eat before Quigley and Manners spread the word around and folks start packing in for a look."

"Suits me," agreed Medford. "The Montezuma?"

"No, Miguel's cantina," Slade answered. "I wish to send word to Pancho Garza to pull in his watchdogs; they're keeping an eye on both ends of the Indian Crossing and will spend the night there unless recalled."

At the cantina, Marie paused for a moment to greet them, then hurried to the back room.

"Got work to do that can't wait," she explained. "We'll talk later."

At Slade's request, Miguel sent word to Pancho and his men. While they were eating, the knife man joined them and was regaled with an account of the day's adventure.

"The eye of *El Halcón* sees all," was his only comment as he accepted a drink and then sauntered to his usual place at the end of the bar.

After they had finished eating and were enjoying a smoke, Slade beckoned him.

"Think you could persuade that cantina owner over in Nuevo Laredo to come to the sheriff's office a little later?" he asked. "I'd like for him to view those bodies."

"*Si,* I will persuade him," Pancho replied cheerfully, tapping the half of his knife. He departed on the errand, leaving his hearers chuckling. Both agreed that Pancho could be quite "persuasive" when he was of a mind to.

Marie joined them and the story was repeated. Her comment was as laconic as Pancho's — "Just a pleasant afternoon's recreation."

A little later Pancho himself entered, with the roly-poly Nuevo Laredo cantina owner in tow.

"I thought it best to bring him here lest he take a notion to escape," explained Pancho, who had a sense of humor.

Slade thought the owner did not look particularly perturbed and made a point of shaking hands cordially with him for the benefit of watching eyes. He willingly accompanied them to the sheriff's office, glanced at the dead faces, and nodded.

"*Si*, two of the *ladrones* of whom I spoke," he said. "*El Capitan* did well!" He listened attentively to the oft-repeated story of what happened and hurried back to his business.

"I've a notion that gent's stock has gone up quite a bit," observed the sheriff. "Means something across the river to be classed as one of *El Halcón's amigos.*"

Folks began dropping in for a look at the bodies. Among the first to arrive was the manager of the stage line, bearing a check which Slade smilingly declined.

"Suppose instead, you make Manners and Quigley a little present," he suggested. "They conducted themselves well and lent a hand at just the right moment."

"I'll do that," the manager promised. "And thank you for everything, Mr. Slade. The loss of that box would have shot our insurance rates up sky-high."

More people came to view the dead outlaws but nobody could recall seeing them anywhere around town. Finally Medford shooed out the last of the curious and shut and locked the door.

"I've a notion those fellers were telling the truth this time," he remarked. "Folks ain't scared of Loco Lobo like they used to be."

"No, but he's liable to quickly do something that will revive their fears, on that you can rely," Slade predicted grimly. "Tobar Shaw never willingly quits; we can expect to hear from him, and soon."

"Must have been a sorta warm go there by the river," the sheriff observed reflectively.

"Yes, it was," Slade acceded. "I don't think I was ever on a hotter spot. Fortunate there were men like Manners and Quigley on that stage; they sailed right in without having to be invited. Must have thrown the devils pretty well off balance; they didn't know which way to turn. In fact, I'm of the opinion it was Manners and Quigley, and one other thing, that saved me."

"One other thing?" the sheriff prompted.

"Yes. Tobar Shaw is a wonderful shot. Even at better than five hundred yards he's deadly. But the sun was low in the sky and slightly to the south. I've a notion the rays dazzled his eyes a bit."

"Uh-huh, and the blue whistlers you were sending around his ears dazzled him a mite, too, I'd say," Medford commented dryly.

"Possibly," Slade admitted. "I know the ones he sent to me were a mite dazzling, especially the last two, one of which clipped a chunk out of my boot heel and the other said 'hello' in my ear as it went past. Well, I think I'll toddle back to the cantina; Marie will be expecting me."

"And I'm going to toddle off to bed," replied the sheriff. "Listening to what happened there by the river makes me as tired as if I was mixed up in it. Getting old, I guess, getting old!"

18

The day passed, and nothing happened. Nothing the local police department couldn't cope with. There were a few friendly knifings, with quick recovery in that clean air. A couple of shootings that did not amount to much, an over abundance of red-eye not calculated to improve the aim, here and there a busted head or some loosened teeth. A dance-floor girl caught her man cheating and lambasted him with a bung-starter. When he came to he promised to do better. But by that time the gal had traipsed off with another gentleman and he was left forlorn.

All good, clean fun, typical of a frontier town on the boom. Walt Slade appreciated the humor of such doings. Rather enjoyed them, in fact. But he did not enjoy the continued lack of activity on the part of the gentleman known as Tobar Shaw, alias Loco Lobo. He experienced a gnawing disquietude, a strengthening premonition that Shaw was building up to something, planning with care in an attempt to avoid another slip-up. And Slade uneasily feared he might do just that, accompanied quite likely with death for one or more innocent persons.

"Perhaps the hellion has pulled out?" suggested Sheriff Medford.

"It is possible, but I don't think so," Slade replied. "If he can manage to make one more big haul, he might."

"Another bank, maybe?"

"Could be," Slade admitted. "Well, all we can do is wait, and keep our eyes and ears open."

"Guess that's right," agreed Medford. "I've a notion we'll hit on something sooner or later." He chuckled.

"Remember that cantina owner over in Nuevo Laredo — Jose Fernando is his name — who did you a favor by spotting that pair of hellions and telling you what they said? Well, by doing you a favor, he did himself one, too, a sorta big one. The word got around how he tipped you off to the sidewinders — I expect he helped spread it — and his business has just about doubled. Folks who wouldn't go in there 'cause the place had a sorta off-color reputation do go in now; he's getting a much better crowd and is cashin' in. Funny how things work out."

Slade looked grave. "That's all very well, but there might be repercussions. Lobo and his bunch won't be feeling overly kind toward him, if they've heard about it, and the chances are they have."

"You figure they might do something to him?" Medford asked.

"It would be like them," Slade replied. "Not only to even the score, but as a warning to others. Something like that would tighten the latigos on jaws in a hurry, latigos that have been loosening up a bit of late."

Medford swore exasperatedly. "Darned if I don't believe you're right again," he said. "I'd never have thought of it, but now you call it to mind, I can see it."

"I'd hate for something to happen to him, and on my account," Slade said. "I'm glad you mentioned the matter." He glanced out the dark window, rolled a cigarette and smoked in thoughtful silence. Abruptly he pinched out the butt and stood up.

"I'm going down to Miguel's place and have a talk with Pancho Garza," he said. "All of a sudden you've got me bothered. Be seeing you a little later."

Slade located the knife man without difficulty and laid the matter before him. Pancho looked thoughtful.

"*Capitan,* I doubt not but you are right," he said. "Such things have happened. And, *Capitan,* this night is a night it could well happen to Fernando. Tonight he will close early, for business will be poor. Tomorrow is a day of great *fiesta.* Tonight people will go to church or stay home to prepare for the feast. There will be few on the streets, and those in the cantinas will not stay long."

"I see," Slade said. "I believe you may have hit it. Suppose we take a walk across the bridge. Wait, get one of your boys, not one of the three who were with you the night I had the ruckus in there with Loco Lobo. We'll take him along with us; I have an idea."

Pancho nodded and sauntered down the bar toward where Miguel stood. Watch though he did, even *El Halcón* was unable to discern to whom he spoke on the way. But after a word or two with Miguel, who remained right where he was, Pancho returned.

"He follows," he said laconically. "Let us go."

Marie was on the dance floor at the moment. Slade waved to her. She waved back, and looked anxious. He and Pancho moseyed out.

They had gone but a short distance when a lithe young man who looked more Yaqui Indian than Mexican glided along beside them.

"Juan," introduced Pancho, who wasted no words. Juan answered *El Halcón's* smile with a flash of white teeth. He also appeared to be on the taciturn side. They crossed the bridge in silence.

Then Slade said, "Juan will go ahead to Fernando's cantina and do a little scouting around and perhaps spot something. You and I, Pancho, will wait in Felipe's place. I don't think it advisable for you and I to enter Fernando's at the moment; we'd be sure to be recognized, and that would give the whole thing away."

"*Si,*" agreed Pancho. "As always, *El Halcón* is wise."

Juan parted company with them and slipped ahead. Slade and Pancho made their way to Felipe's cantina, where they received a warm greeting. Occupying a table with glasses of the owner's most prized wine beside them, they conversed with Felipe, and waited.

Juan was gone some little time, and when he entered, it was so unobtrusively that they did not notice his arrival until he was beside them. He sat down, accepted a glass of wine. Then, without preamble, he said, "Patrons are few. One by one they leave. Two *ladrones* at table, *muy malo ladrones,* drink, and watch, and wait. They watch Fernando. Soon with them will be Fernando, alone."

Juan's English was somewhat peculiar, but succinct and very much to the point. He drained his glass, glanced suggestively at Slade. The Ranger stood up.

"Let's go," he said. "I've a notion there's no time to waste." They waved to Felipe, hurried out and headed for Jose Fernando's cantina, Slade and Pancho walking together, Juan easing along behind them like a laconic ghost.

The street was silent and deserted and Slade set a fast pace. He fervently hoped they were not too late.

"Wait," he breathed as they reached the corner of the building which housed the cantina. Gliding forward another step, he peered cautiously through the smeary window.

Fernando was leaning against the bar, looking frightened. And with good reason. Just rising from a table, the only other occupants of the room, were two men. One held a gun in his hand, the other a long knife.

Slade leaped forward, whisked through the door, Pancho beside him.

"Elevate!" he thundered. "You're covered!"

The man with the gun whirled to face him, the black muzzle jutting forward. Slade drew and shot a split second before he pulled trigger. His bullet fanned the Ranger's face as he fell. At the same instant, Pancho's knife buzzed through the air, and there were two forms on the floor, one still writhing, and choking on the blood that poured from his steel-slashed throat.

Gun ready for instant action, Slade moved forward; but before he reached the two bodies, both were still.

"Practice I need," growled Pancho. "An inch far to the left."

"But not too far, from the looks of him," Slade replied.

Fernando was staring at the prostrate forms with dilated pupils, evidently still very frightened.

"Just in time, *Capitan,* just in time," he said thickly. "One moment more and they would have slain me. *Gracias!*"

"Yes, it was close," Slade conceded, "but ended up as it should, and I don't think you will be bothered again. Incidentally, Pancho it is who deserves your thanks. He provided the information that caused us to move swiftly. Juan, go find the police chief, the *jefe politico,* and bring him here. Fernando, lock the door."

Juan grunted and sped away on the errand. Fernando turned the key.

"He is in the temper that is bad, is Juan," observed Pancho. "To kill he failed to get the chance. Next time, perhaps."

While they waited, Slade sat down and rolled a cigarette. He did not touch the bodies, wanting the chief of police to see things as they were.

Shortly there was a tap on the door. Slade unlocked it to admit Juan and the elderly police chief, whom Slade knew well; they had worked together. The chief extended his hand.

"What do I hear?" he asked, twinkling his shrewd little eyes at Slade. "That two *ladrones* fought and each other slew? Well, well, such things happen in a wicked world. *Capitan,* I joy to find you hale and hearty. You also, Fernando," he added significantly. "Ha! The friends of *El Halcón* live long and prosper. The wine, *si?*"

Slade kept a straight face with difficulty

during this double-talk; the old chief was a card.

Also, however, it was an example of his shrewd and fast thinking and his ability to instantly size up a situation. Slade had no official authority in Mexico and it were best that he not be placed in a position where he would have to answer questions. The chief's explanation of the killings would be accepted without comment; such happenings were commonplace enough in Nuevo Laredo. And the fact that the two men were undoubtedly from the north side of the river would also be considered, with no one regretting their passing, which would be looked upon as good riddance of undesirable specimens.

Fernando poured the wine with a hand that still shook a trifle. The chief emptied his glass with relish and motioned for a refill.

"Now into the pockets we will peer," he said, and proceeded to do so.

"Ha! Many *pesos*," he announced. "The price of a life, no doubt." He shot another significant glance at Fernando, who wet his suddenly dry lips with the tip of his tongue. "I find naught else that one might consider of consequence. You, too, *Capitan?*" Slade agreed the various trinkets were of no significance.

"The money will pay for burying them," he said. "And if you browse around a bit, no doubt you will find a couple of good horses nobody is claiming. Will all help to swell your city treasury."

"Indeed! Indeed!" answered the chief. "A night's work of profit. Ha! *Capitan,* I hope you will see fit to visit us soon again." He chuckled and winked and was undoubtedly hugely enjoying himself. The whole affair was one pleasing to the Latin temperament.

Without compunction, the chief reached down and drew the blood-stained knife from the dead man's throat.

"The remembrance — souvenir, I believe — for Pancho," he said, passing him the blade. "It is good steel. And here is another on the floor, for Juan. They will be useful for the slicing of meat."

The young Mexicans grinned as they accepted the chief's "gift." Pancho wiped his on the dead man's hair and slid it into the sheath where it belonged. The chief, it seemed, had failed to notice that the sheath was empty.

"Once more the wine, Fernando," said the chief. "Then I will arrange for disposal of yon carrion."

"And I guess we'd better be toddling back across the bridge," Slade decided. "Getting late. Thanks for everything, Chief."

"Come again, *Capitan,* and soon," said the chief, pressing his hand. "Here you will ever be welcome."

All in all, not a bad night, Slade reflected as they made their way back to Laredo. They had saved a man's life and deprived Tobar Shaw of two more of his followers; the devil must be scraping the bottom of the barrel. In addition, they had prevented a renewed wave of fear sweeping the riverfront, which was important. Not a bad night.

Sheriff Medford thought so, too, when regaled with an account of the adventure.

"A darn good night," he applauded. "Another big setback for Loco Lobo or Shaw, or whatever you call him. He must be pretty well shook up about now."

"Yes, but because of which he'll be all the more dangerous," Slade pointed out. "A rattlesnake is a timid, peaceful creature that only wishes to escape danger, but corner it and it's vicious and deadly. Tobar Shaw is vicious and deadly at all times, but cornered he'll be even worse. We've still got our work cut out for us."

"We'll do it," the sheriff declared cheerfully. "With you and Pancho and your other Mexican *amigos* on his trail, the hellion ain't got a chance."

However, Slade was inclined to be less optimistic. He was confident that he would finally come out on top in the battle of wits and bullets, but he did not for a moment underestimate Tobar Shaw. Corralling the devil wouldn't be easy. And relax his vigilance and the finish might well be the other way around. Medford voiced a somewhat similar sentiment.

"I've a notion," he said, "that the horned toad is in a frame of mind about now that he wouldn't mind taking the Big Jump just so long as he could take you with him."

"I hope he doesn't succeed," Slade replied smilingly. "I certainly don't desire to spend the hereafter chasing him through eternity. Wouldn't relish it a bit."

"Watch your step or you may end up doing just that," Medford warned. "Don't suppose the devils will bother Fernando again?"

"They'll be sorry if they try it," Slade answered. "I could read between the lines of the old police chief's palaver. Until Loco Lobo is rounded up, Fernando will be guarded by two or three of the same brand as Pancho. We don't have to worry anymore about Fernando."

"Glad to hear that," said the sheriff. "He 'pears to be all right."

"Yes, he is," Slade agreed. "Well, think I'll drop down to Miguel's. I've a notion things will be quiet for the rest of the night."

"Ain't much of it left," Medford grunted. The girls had left the floor and Marie looked very small and lonely at a corner table by herself. She was so glad to see him back safe that she refrained from scolding him.

19

The following day and night were quiet, with no hint of activity on the part of Tobar Shaw, but by which Walt Slade was not lulled into any sense of false security; Shaw would strike again, of that he was convinced, and he endeavored to anticipate what would be the outlaw's next move, and with more hope of doing so than formerly.

Slade felt that his chief accomplishment, so far, was eradicating fear from the minds of many. He knew the true story of what had happened in Jose Fernando's cantina had been quietly passed along, "unofficially," and Shaw's failure to wreak vengeance on Fernando had definitely proven him vulnerable. "Loco Lobo" was no longer the name of terror it had once been, and people who before had been reluctant to talk where the dreaded outlaw leader was concerned would now come forward with any information they might have picked up

— which could well work to Shaw's disadvantage.

His own campaign against the outlaw bunch was steadily gaining force. Pancho and his young men were circulating like hot water, prying, listening, while appearing to do neither. It was a game the Texas-Mexicans with a strong dash of Yaqui blood loved, and the undoubted danger involved only added spice to the adventure. For underneath their veneer civilization was, and not too dormantly, the savage wit of the mountain *Indio* who through untold ages had avoided and confounded murderous foes by similar stratagems and wiles. If there was anything to be learned, they would learn it. And they were proud to be of aid to *El Halcón,* upon whom they looked with veneration. "*El Halcón,* the good, the just, the compassionate! *El Dios,* guard him!"

"Those jiggers are all right," declared Sheriff Medford. "When they're for you, they're for you all the way and no holds barred."

"Yes, there are no better friends," Slade agreed. "Utterly dependable and fiercely loyal."

"So, with all of us working together, maybe we can drop a loop on the sidewinder," concluded Medford. "The big question is, where will the hellion strike next?"

"I don't know, but I'll wager that it will be something to curl our hair for us," Slade predicted.

Walt Slade was definitely right.

Old Eliphalet Hopper's big EH shipping herd was comfortably bedded down on the banks of a little stream. On the north side was a stand of dense and high chaparral that provided an admirable wind break. The cows, full-fed and content, chewed their cuds and rumbled sociably. The night was one of brilliant stars and a thin slice of moon in the west — not too dark.

There had been no widelooping in the section for a long time and scant precautions were taken against such a possibility. Only two night hawks rode slowly around and around the herd, to thwart possible straying. Shortly after daybreak the cows would be shoved to the railroad town and the loading pens, where a buyer awaited them.

The night hawks made a habit of meeting near the stand of chaparral and pausing for a smoke and gab. In half an hour their relief would show up and they would head for the bunkhouse, two miles distant to the east, to grab off a little shut-eye, when they paused together for the last time.

There was the tiniest of rustlings in the growth and a harsh voice barked —

"Up! You're covered!"

The two cowboys didn't hesitate. They didn't like the sound of that voice one bit. Their hands shot into the air. Instantly they were surrounded by four masked men, who ordered them to dismount.

Again they didn't argue the point, knowing well what would very likely be the price paid for disobedience. In a trice they were bound hand and foot with their own tie ropes, gags secured in their mouths. They were shoved to the ground in the shadow of the growth, too far apart to be any possible assistance to each other. Two of the raiders mounted the cowboys' horses, rode to the herd and began circling it. The other two remained beside the brush.

Time passed, not too much of it, and in the distance appeared the two relief hands. They raised a shout as they drew near and saw the two riders circling the herd. An unintelligible reply was called and they rode forward toward the two mounted rustlers who paused near the growth to receive them. And before they realized what was happening, they were staring into gun muzzles.

With dispatch they were treated as had been the first-trick guards. The owlhoots on the ground entered the growth to reappear mounted and leading two riderless horses, to which the other pair transferred. With the raging hands unable to do anything about it, the herd was roused up and started in marching order south by a little west, toward the not too distant Rio Grande. The helpless cowhands' horses were taken along.

The decidedly uncomfortable punchers, craning their heads up from the ground, watched them out of sight.

But once they were well out of sight, the wideloopers called a halt. They transferred their rigs to the four horses bearing the EH brand, tossing the hands' saddles and bridle into a clump of brush, leaving their own mounts to fend for themselves. Then they started the herd once more, but changing course until they headed north by slightly west, toward the railroad town.

It was past daybreak when several EH hands arrived to try and find out why the first-trick night guards hadn't showed up at the bunkhouse. Exclaiming in astonishment at the absence of the herd, they spotted the four trussed-up victims and released them, and were given a profane account of what happened.

A man was sent speeding to the ranch-house to notify Hopper and the other hands, who were already preparing for the drive to the railroad, and to fetch mounts for the four grounded punchers. These, seething with anger over the way they had been duped, vowed their intention of joining in the chase after the wideloopers.

"We may have a chance to catch the blankety-blank-blanks," said Hopper, after he arrived. "They've got a big start, but they've also got a long drive west to where they can ford the river, and those beefs are fat and soft and can't be pushed hard. No tracking 'em over the heavy grass, but down toward the river it's different — grass sparse, ground soft. We oughta be able to pick up the trail there. Let's go!"

They went like the devil pounding tanbark. Nearing the river, they ranged far and wide, and found nothing. They even crossed the stream at the point, far to the west, where it could be forded, and questioned folks on the south shore.

Nobody recalled seeing a herd of wet cows, or if they did, they did not choose to say so. With the sun low in the west, the thoroughly disgusted outfit gave up and headed for home, to find one devil of a surprise awaiting them.

20

The EH shipping herd rolled into the railroad town shortly before mid-morning. The waiting buyer was favorably impressed by the rather commonplace but gentlemanly and courteous individual who identified himself as Rance Duret, the new EH range boss. He mentioned the former boss by name, explaining that he had decided to quit working for wages and was going into business for himself — which, the buyer recalled, he had been talking about doing for some time.

The buyer, with a contract to fill, was anxious to get the stock moving, so the weighing-in was expedited and the cows shoved through the loading pens and into the waiting stock cars with dispatch. The buyer paid for the herd in cash, a very large sum, as Hopper, who didn't care for checks, insisted on.

"Don't remember seeing those four

punchers before," somebody remarked.

"Oh, Hopper has been doing quite a bit of hiring of late, like the other spreads," a companion replied. "With the irrigation folks in need of workers and paying big, quite a few of the boys have been joining up with 'em for a spell. Can make more money in a week than by following a cow's tail for a month. Can't blame 'em." Which was a readily accepted explanation of the four strangers riding horses bearing the EH brand.

The loading was quickly completed, an engine coupled on, and the cars loaded with EH beefs rolled east. The buyer shared the caboose with the train crew.

The four "EH hands" rode out of town, headed in the direction of the EH casa.

It was well past dark when Eliphalet Hopper and three of his hands, including Jim Carroway, his range boss, stormed into town. Ensued utter confusion and hell on wheels. A cowboy from one of the northern spreads had paused at the EH ranchhouse for a bite before continuing on his way and had casually mentioned that the shipping herd was rolling on its way. Explanations were forthcoming, and Hopper understood.

A wire was dispatched, requesting the

stock train to be held at the next stop. Carroway himself raced to Laredo to brief Sheriff Medford on the details of the outrage and to inform him that it was Hopper's opinion that the wideloopers had headed in his direction. Hopper cursed everybody and everything, including the day he was born.

"The nerve of that sidewinder!" Medford raved to Walt Slade. "Did you ever hear the like? Wideloop a herd, drive it to town and sell it to the legitimate buyer under everybody's nose! You told me about the hellion stealing the oil well over at Beaumont, but this is even better."

"Yes, the gent at his best," Slade replied. "Never misses a bet. Has all the details at his fingertips before he starts to move. He familiarized himself with everything concerning the EH spread and then struck." He turned to Carroway.

"By the way, have you had any visitors of late?" he asked. Carroway pondered a moment.

"Yep, come to think of it, we did," he answered. "A sorta nice appearin' jigger who said his name was Duret and that he aimed to buy a spread in the section if he could find one with the price right. Asked a lot of questions about the cow business hereabouts."

"And I imagine in the course of the conversation, he learned when your shipping herd would be shoved to town?" Slade prodded.

"Yep, guess he did," nodded Carroway. "He asked about shippin' facilities hereabouts and dependable buyers. Hopper told him when we aimed to roll the herd and that if he'd make a point of being in town that day he'd meet him there and introduce him to a buyer he could depend on."

"He made a point of being in town, all right, but evidently Hopper didn't meet him," Slade observed dryly. "And I suppose he also learned where the cows would be held in close herd prior to the day of shipment?"

"Right again," Carroway admitted. "Him and the Old Man rode out to where we were getting the herd together and looked 'em over. Feller 'lowed Hopper sure knew good stock, which sorta pleased the Old Man. He was quite took with the feller."

"And got took," growled Medford.

"So you see how he worked it," Slade said to the sheriff. "Even to changing horses and riding those bearing EH burns."

"Wonder why he didn't cash in those four

hands?" said the sheriff. "That wasn't like him."

"For two reasons, I'd say," Slade replied. "For one thing, on a still night a shot can be heard a long ways, with maybe the wrong pair of ears catching the sound — he takes everything into consideration. Secondly, he wished them to see which way the herd was driven, so that they would naturally come to the conclusion that it was being shoved across the Rio Grande — which was just how it worked out."

"And the chance that horned toad took!" snorted Medford. "Somebody might have been around who knew well Jim here hadn't quit and Hopper hadn't hired those hands."

"Not too much of a chance," Slade answered. "With the four of them forking horses with the EH burn, unless it was somebody from the EH outfit, nobody would give the matter much thought. In fact, it is fortunate nobody did catch on. Then the buyer would have been killed, his poke lifted, and the devils would have shot their way out of town, very likely killing somebody else."

"Guess you're right," conceded Medford. "Blazes! What a tangle! The hellions have the buyer's money, the buyer has Hopper's cows. They'll be fighting it out in the courts for the next five years, trying to figure who did what to who and who gets paid for it. That cunning devil!"

"Say!" exclaimed Carroway, "who is it you fellers keep talking about?"

"Oh, a nice sociable gent known hereabouts as Loco Lobo," Slade explained. Carroway jumped in his chair.

"Holy hoptoads!" he sputtered. "You mean one of those hellions was that killer?"

"Yes, Loco Lobo, minus his disguise, which consists of a darkened skin and a big nose and darkened hair," Slade replied.

"Holy hoptoads!" Carroway repeated. "Wait till the boys he tied up hear who it was. They'll shiver like a dog sitting on a cactus spine."

"With reason," Slade agreed. "The only reason they are alive is that it suited Lobo's convenience; he considered them more valuable alive than dead, at the moment. As the Karankawa Indians would say, their spirits looked in their direction last night. Well, Lobo made his strike and he's well heeled with *dinero* again."

"Maybe the vinegaroon will lay off for a while," hazarded the sheriff.

"I doubt it," Slade answered. "He has a devil of restlessness that keeps him on the move. He's not happy unless he's pulling something."

"Maybe he might pull out of the section?"

"It is possible," Slade admitted. "Well, we can only wait and see. However, I have a hunch we'll be hearing from him in some fashion or other, soon."

After Carroway had departed for bed, the sheriff remarked, "Notice you didn't mention Shaw while Jim was here."

"The fewer who know I have recognized Loco Lobo as Tobar Shaw the better," Slade explained. "In fact, I am not at all sure that Shaw himself realizes I have penetrated his disguise; I hope he doesn't."

"But he must have recognized you as the man who's caused him so much trouble," said Medford.

"Naturally," Slade answered. "He could hardly do otherwise. But that doesn't really matter, so far as I can see."

"Except it makes him doubly anxious to get rid of you," Medford grumbled.

"His eagerness may cause him to do something impulsive, which won't work to his advantage," Slade said.

"Uh-huh, but I don't like it," snorted Medford. "That snake-blooded devil gives me the jitters." Slade laughed, and changed the subject.

"I almost hope he would pull out," Medford interrupted. "Maybe he has."

Although he did not think so, as uneventful days passed, Slade began to wonder, a bit uneasily, if Medford could be right in his surmise that Tobar Shaw, after making his good haul, would pull out of the section; it began to look a little that way. Slade spent much of his time, when he wasn't prowling about Laredo, at the sheriff's office, for Pancho and his young men were continually combing both towns in the hope of hitting on something significant.

And then, on the fifth day, when the Ranger was begining to develop a decidedly pessimistic frame of mind, Pancho dropped in casually, as was his wont, occupied a chair and rolled a husk *cigaro.* Slade waited patiently for him to speak.

"Capitan," he said at length, when the smoke was going to his satisfaction, *"Capitan,* you doubtless remember the four *ladrones* who waited to kill you in the saloon of Carter, my *amigo."*

"I'm not likely to forget them, nor the part you played in that ruckus," Slade replied. "Why?"

Instead of answering the question, Pancho countered with one of his own, "And you will recall that one escaped, *si?"*

"Yes, streaked through the door before we could line sights with him," Slade replied, and repeated, "Why?"

"Because, *Capitan*," Pancho replied sententiously, "tonight I saw that one accursed. On the street in Nuevo Laredo. Me he did not see. Him I followed, and my blade was hungry. He entered a cantina of evil repute. Through the window I saw him sit at table with three others. The table was close to an open window, beyond which was a dark alley. The alley I entered and stood where I could see and not be seen. Two of those at table with him were *ladrones* like himself. The third was different; he dressed in what you call store clothes, and his voice was soft."

"Can you describe him?" Slade asked eagerly.

"*Capitan*," Pancho replied, "there is little to describe. He was a hombre ordinary, the kind one passes on the street without seeing. He looked to be a mild and courteous gentleman, save for his eyes. Those eyes, *Capitan*, were with fire filled — fire under ice — the lidless eyes of a snake."

"Tobar Shaw, sure as blazes!" Slade exclaimed. "Yes, Loco Lobo minus his disguise. What next?"

"They talked together, their voices very

low," Pancho resumed. "I tried to hear what was said, but I could hear little. Only scattered words that were meaningless. I did hear Loco Lobo say what sounded like 'The night after tomorrow night.' And, very clearly, 'Rio Grande City.' Does it mean aught to you?"

"Frankly, I don't know just what it means," Slade said. "May be very important. Sounds like they plan something in Rio Grande City. What did they do?"

"Very shortly they left the cantina," replied Pancho. "They mounted *caballos* hitched to the rack in front of the cantina — I moved to the corner and watched. They rode west on the Camino Real."

"The old trail that parallels the river, in Mexico," Slade observed musingly. "They did not ride east by south toward Rio Grande City."

"That is so," said Pancho.

"But it sounds like they aim to be there the night after tomorrow night."

"*Si.*"

"It was Loco Lobo, all right," Slade repeated. "No doubt about it; your description of his eyes was perfect. Yes, Tobar Shaw as his normal self."

"So I felt, *Capitan,*" Pancho agreed.

For some time Slade sat deep in thought.

Finally he said, "No sense in us making a move before tomorrow night. Scout around, Pancho, and maybe you can learn something more. I'll give Laredo a once-over tomorrow." The Mexican nodded, and slipped out. Slade waited until the sheriff arrived and repeated what Pancho told him.

"So it looks like we will head for Rio Grande City tomorrow night," he concluded. "What we'll do when we get there, I have no idea, but it seems the logical thing to do."

"I figure you're right," agreed Medford, "but I've got no official authority down there."

"I'll deputize you and Pancho," Slade promised. "We'll have to take him along; be heartbroken if we don't."

"And he's a good man to have along," said the sheriff. "Okay, it'll be a long ride, but we should be able to make it in time."

"Yes, I think so," Slade agreed. "With a lay-over of a few hours at Zapata, to rest the cayuses, and perhaps another hour at Roma."

The following afternoon, Slade prowled Laredo, but with little hope of discovering anything of value. Gradually he worked his way to the river. Tied up at the dock was a big river steamer. Not many of the big ones reached Laredo anymore, but now and then one did. He gazed at it idly. Then abruptly he leaned forward, staring with narrowed eyes. The name of the ship was stenciled on its side; it read —

Rio Grande City!

21

For a moment Slade gazed, his mind working at racing speed. Then he turned and hurried to the sheriff's office, where Medford was working at his desk.

"Well," he announced, "we won't take a long and hard ride tonight. Instead, tomorrow night we'll treat ourselves to a nice comfortable jaunt down the river."

"Now what the devil are you talking about?" the sheriff demanded peevishly. Slade ignored the question.

"I believe the company owning that big steamer down at the dock, along with a lot of others, has an agent here, has it not?" he asked.

"Sure," replied Medford. "What of it?"

"I wish to have a little talk with that agent," Slade answered. "Just for your edification, the name on that steamer happens to be *Rio Grande City.* Beginning to catch on?"

Medford stared with dawning comprehension. "I guess I am," he said. "Let's go! Feller's name is Wing, Earl Wing; he's all right."

The agent proved to be a middle-aged, affable gentleman. After they were introduced, Slade studied him a moment, decided he was not a person addicted to loose talking, and arrived at a decision. From a cunningly concealed secret pocket in his broad leather belt, he produced something that he laid on the desk before the agent. Wing stared at the gleaming silver star set on a silver circle, the feared and honored badge of the Texas Rangers!

"Mr. Wing," Slade said as he restored the badge to its hiding place, "I trust you can be discreet. Forget what you just saw. Now I'd like to ask you a few questions. First, I assume that your steamer anchored at the dock will be packing a considerable bit of money down river tomorrow night. Is that right?"

The agent stared, hesitated.

"Come across, Earl," the sheriff advised.

"Yes, it is," Wing admitted. "A very large sum, nearly eighty thousand dollars, consigned from the Laredo bank to the Brownsville bank. You don't think —"

"I don't think, I know," Slade interrupted.

"Somewhere between here and Brownsville an attempt will be made to rob your steamer, very likely accompanied by a loss of life if it is not thwarted. Are you carrying any passengers this trip?"

"Why, yes," the agent said. "This morning a gentleman booked passage to Brownsville for himself and three companions."

"Can you describe him?" Slade asked.

"Well, he was a rather ordinary looking person, tall, with a pleasant voice and sorta yellow hair. That's about all I recall about him. Do you know who he is?"

"I do," Slade answered. "A gentleman known hereabouts as Loco Lobo."

The agent jumped in his chair. "That robber and killer?" he gasped. "Sheriff, why don't you arrest him?"

"Because we have nothing for which to arrest him," Slade replied for Medford. "Although we know he is Loco Lobo, we couldn't prove it. I trust," he added grimly, "that it will be a different story tomorrow night. Now here's what I wish you to do.

"Smuggle us aboard the steamer tonight and hole us up where we won't be seen. You must take the captain into your confidence, of course, but nobody else. Can you arrange it?"

"I can," the agent replied energetically.

"Tonight the men will be given shore leave and there will be nobody left on the vessel save a watchman. The money will not be delivered until tomorrow and the safe in the captain's cabin will not be guarded, of course. I can arrange with the captain that an absolutely discreet and dependable man will fill the role of watchman; he'll take care of you. Do you think it safe to have that money delivered to the steamer, Mr. Slade?"

"You'll have nothing to worry about," the Ranger promised. After a look at him, Wing decided it was so.

"However, if you are uneasy about it, you can have dummy packages delivered from the bank, only that will mean taking others in your confidence and there might be a slip, for it's fairly certain one of the devils is keeping tabs on the shipment," Slade added.

"The bank is anxious for that shipment to reach Brownsville without delay, so we'll take a chance," the agent answered cheerfully. "I am confident it will be amply protected."

"Thank you," Slade smiled. "So we'll meet here in your office shortly after dark, okay?"

"That will be fine," said Wing, "and thank you, Mr. Slade, for everything."

"By your cooperation, you will be helping to rid the section of an infernal pest," Slade complimented the agent as they rose to go. Mr. Wing looked very pleased.

That night the maneuver was executed without a hitch. The watchman proved to be an old colored man who announced he was also the cook. He shrewdly singled out Slade as the leader of the party and addressed his remarks to him as he ushered them into the captain's deck cabin, which was large.

"And you don't have to bother about going hungry tomorrow, Boss Man," he said. "The captain's a big eater and nobody can tell how much vittles I got on a covered tray. The feller who was supposed to stand watch today was glad to trade places with me. I told him I was feelin' sorta poorly and didn't hanker for any drinking. Captain told him it would be all right. And if you have trouble with those rapscallions you're waitin' for, I got a nice big meat cleaver in my galley, and I can use it."

"Thank you," Slade replied. "Might come in handy, never can tell. Your name?"

"I'm called Uncle Zeke," introduced the colored man. Slade supplied his own name and those of his companions and they shook hands.

Glancing around the cabin, Slade was pleased with the layout. The cabin was commodious and comfortably furnished with a table and chairs secured to the deck. There were two bunks in a tier and he saw that holed up behind the end of the tier, they would be out of sight from the door. In one corner stood a big iron safe. On the far side was another door.

"Where does that lead to?" he asked Uncle Zeke.

"I'll show you, Boss Man," the cook replied. "It's always kept locked." He turned a key and opened the door, which led to a dark and narrow passage between the cabin wall and the rail. Beside the door was a small window. All the windows were heavily curtained.

"Will be fine for our purpose," Slade told Uncle Zeke as he closed and locked the door.

A number of blankets were stacked on one of the bunks, and sleeping on the floor posed no problem for those hardy campaigners.

"Nobody comes in here," said Uncle Zeke. "Marse Captain don't 'low it, and he don't stand for no foolishment. You'll be plumb snug here and nothing to bother about. I'll fetch a pot of coffee and some sandwiches for a snack." He proceeded to do so.

"Here's how I figure their plan," Slade said to the others. "I'm of the opinion they'll attempt to pull off the robbery between here and San Ygnacio, about thirty miles southeast of Laredo. They'll have horses cached on the Mexican side of the river. They would force the steamer's crew to land them there, on the Mexican shore, where nobody lives. Grabbing off the horses they'd head into Mexico. I suspect the three hellions with Shaw wouldn't live very long; the snake-blooded devil would manage to do away with them and make for the interior of Mexico with all the loot. He'd be sitting pretty, for eighty thousand dollars is a hefty passel of *dinero.*"

"Think they'll have somebody watching the horses?" asked Medford.

"I don't think so," Slade answered. "I believe the three who will board the ship with Shaw are all that's left of his bunch. The horses will be hobbled where there is grass and water, hidden in the brush. I could be wrong, but I don't think I am. I figure that's the way they'll work it."

"And I figure you're right," said Medford. "Say, these sandwiches are prime. Uncle Zeke, you're some cook, along with being a first rate fightin' man."

"Thank you, suh," replied Uncle Zeke,

with a flash of teeth startlingly white in his black face.

Slade examined the safe. It was of ancient vintage.

"That box would pose no difficulty to Tobar Shaw," he announced. "He'd have it open in three minutes."

Around midnight the captain put in an appearance, a hard-bitten old salt, a former deep-water man. Slade felt sure he was dependable; he seemed to rather enjoy the prospect in view.

"Make yourself comfortable," he said. "I'll see you later, after I get those lubbers of a crew tucked in their bunks; they'll be dropping anchor here before long."

The night passed comfortably enough, and without incident, as did the following day. Shortly after noon, the money from the bank arrived. The captain received the sacks while standing in the door and passed them to Uncle Zeke, who stowed them in the safe and clanged the door shut. The captain signed a receipt and winked at Slade.

Meanwhile, Slade had, with the aid of a pair of trousers and one of the captain's coats, contrived an artful dummy. When it was seated in a chair, back to the door, with a cap on top, it was, in the rather dim light, a creditable simulacrum of the captain leaning forward over the table.

Just before dark the captain appeared again. "They just came aboard," he announced in a whisper. "I assigned them to two cabins down at the stern. We used to get a lot of passengers, before the railroad came along, and ample provision was made for them. Those four devils all went into one cabin and shut the door and pulled the curtains."

"Fine," Slade told him. "I believe everything is going to work out."

The captain nodded and hurried off, to reappear a little later.

"Well, here we go," he said. "Guess I'd better stay in here, out of sight."

"That's right," Slade replied. "Take it easy."

A windlass creaked and whined, then the throb of the engines vibrated the ship. The paddle-wheels beat the water and the *Rio Grande City* moved down the river.

Slade waited half an hour and a little more, then motioned to his companions. Unlocking the back door, they stepped out into the dark passage. Slade closed the door, stationed himself beside the little window. The voices of the crew and the activities of the vessel putting out from port sounded loud through the still air. Lounging comfortably against the cabin wall, he waited.

He didn't have long to wait. Abruptly, the other door opened and four figures glided in. Slade instantly recognized the foremost as Tobar Shaw.

There was the gleam of a knife as Shaw struck; the blade buried in the "captain's" back, or what Shaw took to be the captain. The dummy, not unnaturally, fell to the floor. Shaw uttered a startled exclamation.

Flinging open the door, Slade stepped into the cabin. His voice rang out —

"Trail's end, Shaw! Up, you're covered!"

Tobar Shaw whirled at the sound of his voice. His left hand flashed across his middle in a deadly cross-pull. But Slade's Colt boomed the instant before Shaw pulled trigger. His bullet ripped a welt along the top of Slade's shoulder and hurled him sideways. He continued to shoot, the slugs hammering Shaw's body. Shaw fell forward on his face.

An arc of flame streaked across the cabin, and Pancho's knife had claimed another victim. The sheriff was blazing away. Answering lead screeched through the air, but the outlaws, completely demoralized, fired wildly. Slade shot with both hands. Then he lowered his smoking guns and peered through the powder fog at the motionless forms on the floor. His gaze centered on Tobar Shaw. The outlaw leader, the terrible Loco Lobo, lay on his face, his life draining out through the bullet holes in his chest. Slade knelt beside him and gently turned him over on his back. Shaw's glazing eyes glared up at him with hellish hate. Words seeped through his blood-frothing lips.

"You win, damn you!" he gasped. "But what do you get out of it?"

"Nothing, Shaw, except the satisfaction of a chore well done," *El Halcón* answered. He held the star of the Rangers before the dying outlaw's eyes. Shaw stared at it.

"If — if I'd known you — were — a Ranger," he panted, "I'd never have come — back — to — Texas." His chest arched as he fought for air, fell in. It did not rise again.

Walt Slade straightened and gazed down at the dead man. As more than once before, a wave of sadness swept over him. Why couldn't so able a brain have been turned to a good purpose!

"His lust for murder was his undoing," Slade said to Medford. "He was lightning fast and might have shaded me; but his left hand wasn't quite as fast as his right; in which he held the knife." He turned to the captain, beside whom Uncle Zeke stood, with a big cleaver in his hand.

"Well, sir, I guess you'd better turn your ship around and head back to Laredo, so we can dispose of the bodies," he said. "Then you can proceed on your way to Brownsville, with your money safe."

"Yes, safe, thanks to you, Mr. Slade," the skipper answered. He stared at the dummy resting peacefully beside the bodies and, tough old sailorman though he was, he shuddered.

"And if it wasn't for you, *that* would have been me," he replied thickly. "Much obliged again."

Later, Slade and Medford sat in the sheriff's office and contemplated the stark forms laid out for display.

"Pancho will send some of his boys to free those horses of their hobbles and bring them in, which will take care of everything," Slade observed.

"And now what?" the sheriff asked.

"And now I'm ambling down to Miguel's cantina," Slade answered. "Tobar Shaw is dead, and this time I think he'll stay dead, and my chore here is finished. I believe I'll treat myself to a few days of the vacation I so far haven't had."

Some days later, Marie said gaily, "Be seeing you, after you've made the rounds."

With a smile on her lips and tears on her

lashes, she watched him ride away, tall and graceful atop his great black horse, to answer the call of duty and face danger and new adventure.

We hope you have enjoyed this Large Print book. Other Thorndike, Wheeler, and Chivers Press Large Print books are available at your library or directly from the publishers.

For information about current and upcoming titles, please call or write, without obligation, to:

Publisher
Thorndike Press
295 Kennedy Memorial Drive
Waterville, ME 04901
Tel. (800) 223-1244

or visit our Web site at:

www.gale.com/thorndike
www.gale.com/wheeler

OR

Chivers Large Print
published by BBC Audiobooks Ltd
St James House, The Square
Lower Bristol Road
Bath BA2 3SB
England
Tel. +44(0) 800 136919
email: bbcaudiobooks@bbc.co.uk
www.bbcaudiobooks.co.uk

All our Large Print titles are designed for easy reading, and all our books are made to last.